Whoops!

"I think we should invite most of the people in our home-room and then ..." Frowning, Lacy paused for a second. "Oh, do either of you know that little crippled girl who came in?" She put a hand to her mouth, barely touching her lips with the tips of her fingers. "Whoops, maybe I should say handicapped, instead of crippled."

I nodded my agreement. "I think you're right, Lacy. That is a better term than crippled."

Next to me Brandy cleared her throat.

"Like, both of you are totally out of touch. The current, politically correct expression is 'physically challenged.'"

"The best word is Judy." A soft, pleasant voice made all three of us stop and spin around. Judy Baird was right behind us. She didn't stop or even look in our direction when she added: "But if Judy is too hard for you to remember, crippled or handicapped is fine. It doesn't matter."

Books by Bill Wallace

Red Dog
Trapped in Death Cave

Available from ARCHWAY Paperbacks

Beauty
The Biggest Klutz in Fifth Grade
Blackwater Swamp
Buffalo Gal
The Christmas Spurs
Danger in Quicksand Swamp
Danger on Panther Peak
(Original title: Shadow on the Snow)
A Dog called Kitty
Ferret in the Bedroom, Lizards in the Fridge
Never Say Quit
Snot Stew
Totally Disgusting!
True Friends
Watchdog and the Coyotes

Available from MINSTREL Books

BILL WALLACE

True Friends

A
MINSTREL®
BOOK

Published by POCKET BOOKS
New York   London   Toronto   Sydney   Tokyo   Singapore

A Minstrel book published by
POCKET BOOKS, a division of Simon & Schuster Inc.
1230 Avenue of the Americas, New York, NY 10020

Copyright © 1994 by Bill Wallace

Published by arrangement with Holiday House, Inc.

ISBN: 0-671-53036-4

10 9 8 7 6 5 4 3 2 1

A MINSTREL BOOK and colophon are registered trademarks of
Simon and Schuster Inc.

Cover art by Dan Duffy

Printed in the U.S.A.

With admiration to Julie (Nixon) Ferrell, whose courage and determination were my inspiration for this story

CHAPTER

1

The motor roared. Then it coughed and sputtered. It was a weak cough, kind of like a first grader faking a cold. The fresh morning scent of honeysuckle that followed me when I walked through the little garden between the house and the garage was instantly chased from my head. The strong smell of gasoline and burning oil replaced the sweet odor. After a faint groaning sound, the car engine died.

I sighed and propped my elbows on the radiator. I peeked through the crack above the motor housing and beneath the back of the raised hood. I could see the windshield. Daddy was leaning down, his nose almost touching the steering wheel, and peeking back at me.

"What do you think?" he called from inside the little Corvette.

I glanced at the breather, then back through the crack at him.

"Sounds like the carburetor."

Daddy winked at me and smiled. "Think you're right." He pulled the key from the ignition and got out. In a second, he joined me at the front of the car. He leaned on the fender and looked at the motor. "Think I should pick up a new carburetor kit from the shop and give it a try?"

I smiled up at him.

"Courtney, where are you? We're going to be late."

The sound of Emily's voice cracked against the stillness. I didn't answer.

"Then again," he suggested, "it could be the pistons."

I shrugged and pushed a wisp of blond hair off my forehead. "I figure we're gonna have to change out the carburetor anyway. If we do that first, and it still won't start . . ."

"Courtney? You're not out there with your dad, are you? Courtney?"

My stepmother's voice, as high and shrill as the sound of fingernails being scraped on a chalkboard, was closer now. Daddy nudged me with his elbow. "Scoot, before she . . ."

"Courtney Ann Brown!" Right behind me,

Emily's voice bit the summer morning. "You get away from that car. You get grease on your new wraparound skirt and the stitched vest I got you and I'll . . ."

I turned to face her. I held my hands out and looked down. "I didn't touch anything, Mother. I was just looking. See? Clean and white as when you brought it home."

I didn't like calling Emily "Mother." But a year and a half ago, when she and Daddy got married, she'd insisted on it. And, if it made Daddy happy . . . well . . .

Emily looked me up and down. Her lip curled up on one side of her face, and her eyebrow arched. She shook her head.

"Can't believe it." She sighed. "I arrange for Maggie to come in early for your hair appointment. I get you a brand-new skirt and vest for the first day of school. New white Cole-Haan sandals. And what do you do? Sneak out here and tromp around in the grease and crud. Now come on, we're going to be late for your beauty appointment."

My shoulders sagged when I turned. Emily trotted off toward her car. I hesitated a second and spun to face Daddy. Another strand of blond hair flopped across my eye. I brushed it aside with my thumb.

"After school?"

Daddy shook his head. "Coach Bentley wants me to drop by the football field and talk with him about your brother. Figured I'd watch Ben practice a few minutes while I was there."

"Ben's not in trouble, is he?"

Dad shrugged. "Don't know what's going on with Ben. Whatever Coach wants to talk to me about, it'll be late when I get home. How about we work over the curburetor after supper?"

"After supper," I agreed.

"Courtney! Right this instant!" Emily barked. "Maggie has other clients. If we don't make it to your appointment, your hair's going to look like a rag mop. You don't want to look like some little bag lady on the first day at your new school, do you? Now hurry!"

"Yes, Mother."

When it came to smells, flowers had to be my favorite. Honeysuckle was real high up on the list. Roses and lilacs and stuff like that were pretty good, too. Next came Vel soap, followed by the smell of oil and gasoline. And way, *way* down at the bottom of my smell list was the stink that came from a beauty shop.

I figured all this out while I was sitting under the hair dryer in Maggie's Magic Shears.

After Maggie'd shampooed my hair and rolled it on these little tiny, pink rollers, she'd stuck me under the dryer. My hair was wrapped so tight, my head hurt. I felt like my whole scalp was stretched up an inch or two. I pinched my nose shut. If I breathed through my mouth, I could block out the smell of the beauty shop so I could think about nice smells.

Once, I'd asked Daddy about the honeysuckle in the little garden between the house and the garage. He'd told me that my mother had planted the bushes and the ones outside my bedroom window as well. "The first summer we moved into the house, she started a garden. She loved flowers," he'd told me. "She always had vases filled with fresh flowers from her garden. You sure take after your mother when it comes to flowers."

Vel soap, I figured out on my own. It was what my mother used.

Mama died when I was real little. I hardly remember her. Except for the photograph on my dresser and the ones Daddy has in his scrapbook, I couldn't even picture what she looked like.

Mostly my memories of Mama were feelings.

I remember how soft she was. I remember how she used to run her fingers lightly over my face—tickling my skin until I'd close my eyes and fall asleep. I can't remember the sound of her voice, but I can remember how warm and safe and peaceful I felt when she curled up next to me and read a bedtime story. And . . . I remember her clean, fresh smell. I'd all but forgotten it. Daddy took me grocery shopping one day, when I was about five or so. He was hunting for this stuff called Lava. It was a kind of soap that got the oil and dirt off his hands when he was finished at the garage. We were in the soap aisle and this smell kind of tugged at my nose.

Then it kind of tugged at my heart.

I picked a bar of Vel soap from the rack and held it up to Daddy.

"Mama?"

I still remember the look on his face. It was a sad, almost hurt look. For a second it seemed like little pools of water collected at the bottom of his eyes. Then he smiled down at me and nodded.

"Yes, hon," he said, "that's what your mama used."

I brushed the back of my hand under my nose like I was scratching my upper lip. Really, I was smelling the Vel soap.

Maybe I *was* growing up, like Emily said. Maybe one day I'd have a house filled with fresh flowers from my garden. Maybe I'd smell of Vel soap and be kind and gentle and soft and warm and . . .

Suddenly Maggie was standing beside me. She'd shut off the dryer and lifted the big, bowl-shaped thing up from my head. I yanked my hand from my nose and lay it in my lap.

"You're done." She smiled, touching my hair. "After I brush you out and use a little hair spray, Courtney Brown's going to be the prettiest young lady in junior high."

I followed her back to the chair. I hadn't noticed Lacy Valentine come in. I guess I was all wrapped up in my memories of Mama. Lacy smiled and fluttered her eyelashes.

"I'm having a big back-to-school party, Courtney. Will you help me decide who to invite and help me call people?"

I thought I was going to die!

CHAPTER

2

"Oh, Courtney," Brandy swooned from the desk behind me in Mrs. Hooper's first-hour homeroom. "I mean, like having Lacy Valentine ask you to help plan her party—like that's to die for. How supercool radical!"

Some of the other kids in the room were starting to turn and look in our direction. I scooted down in my chair and shot Brandy a look, trying to shush her.

"Like, you will put me on the list, won't you?" Brandy asked, even louder. "I mean, like I am your best friend and you won't forget Alyson and . . ."

"Brandy." I put a finger to my lips.

". . . and Theresa Dayton," she went on, completely ignoring me. "No, Lacy will invite Theresa. Beth Simms would like to be invited, and . . ."

"Brandy!"

She glanced around. There weren't many kids in the room, but almost all of them were staring at us. Brandy smiled sheepishly and leaned forward in her chair.

"Until you started dressing so cool and your mom started having your hair done every week, Lacy wouldn't even speak to us. Now, she's asking you to help plan her party. That's like the ultimate. You don't know how lucky you are to have Emily for a mom."

I felt a cold chill race up my spine.

"I mean, like she buys you gorgeous clothes. She takes you to the beauty shop. Lets you wear makeup if you want. You got your ears pierced in fourth grade. Like, how radical."

I turned around again to glare at her. Brandy propped her elbow on her desk and rested her chin in her hand.

"My mom probably won't let me get my ears pierced until I'm out of college. She thinks Cole-Haans are something you get from staying out in the snow too long." She laughed. "Get it?"

I frowned at her.

"Like you know, Cole-Haans . . . Cole Feet . . . get it . . . from playing in the snow?"

I got it, I just didn't think it was all that funny. Brandy shrugged off my blank stare.

"Anyway," she continued, "the stuff she drags

home for me to wear looks like it came from a secondhand store. I'd die for something out of the J. Crew catalog." She sighed and looked longingly out the window. "I'm gonna have to be married and have my own family before she even thinks about letting me grow up. You've got it made."

There was a rustling sound near the doorway. I glanced up. Larry Don Perdue leaped over his desk and slid into his seat.

"She's coming!" he announced in a loud whisper.

Since second grade, Larry Don and I had always been in the same room. And since second grade, Larry Don had always been the lookout. Every year he sat in the seat closest to the door so he could keep track of what went on in the halls. Mainly, it was so he could warn the rest of the room when the teacher was coming.

Greg Bowlin, who I'd been stuck in the same room with since fourth grade, and a new kid named Joshua Kemp were scuffling at the back of the room. When Larry Don barked out his whispered warning, they stopped their wrestling and slipped into their seats.

I turned to face the front of the room. Putting both feet on the floor, I smoothed my new wraparound.

A tall lady with glasses came through the doorway. We looked like the model class. Everyone sat up straight and proper. Mrs. Hooper smiled at us, then walked briskly to her desk at the front of the room.

"Wish my folks could afford to send me to the beauty shop the first day of school. That would be to die for." Brandy shot one last whisper at me. "Like we just can't afford it."

A little twinge of worry and guilt rippled through my stomach. "We can't either," I thought to myself, only I didn't say anything.

Mrs. Hooper plucked a new long piece of chalk from the tray at the chalkboard and started writing.

Mrs. Hooper
Sixth Grade English
First Period (Homeroom)
8:05–9:10

There was no use saying anything to Brandy. If I told her what my brother had said about Daddy having to go to the bank to borrow money, she'd have it all over school that we were broke. We really weren't, but there was no sense trying to explain that to Brandy. "Lots of people borrow money." That's what Emily said. "You have to have money to make money."

As for me, I didn't know beans about money. I did know that having my hair done every week cost a lot. But maybe Brandy *was* right. After all, she was probably the brightest kid in the whole school. Listening to her talk, most people would never guess. Ever since her mom and dad divorced and she started spending summers in California, she sounded like a regular dingbat. It seemed as if she started every sentence with "like" and she was always saying "to die for" or "radical." Still, when it came to school, Brandy was a regular genius. So . . . maybe she *was* right. Maybe getting my hair done was worth it.

Mrs. Hooper sat at her desk and picked up a long sheet of computer paper. I could tell it was computer paper because it had green stripes across it and holes all up and down the sides. She peeked over the paper at us.

"It appears that only about half our class is here. The others must still be stuck in the office. We'll wait awhile before I try to take roll or go over any of the orientation materials. You may visit, quietly, while we're waiting."

Instantly, I heard a clunking sound behind me. I glanced over my left shoulder. Greg Bowlin shoved Joshua. Joshua pushed him back, almost knocking him out of his chair.

"I said *'visit!'*" Mrs. Hooper barked from the front of the room. "Not scuffle."

Joshua gave her an innocent grin. Then he folded his arms on top of his desk and laid his head on them.

Three more people came through the door. They looked around, kind of dumb and confused for a moment, then found desks and sat down.

There were about fifteen people in the room now. I knew Brandy, Larry Don, Greg, and the name of the new kid, Joshua. The others—I had no idea who they were. Two other elementary schools besides West sent students to Blyle for sixth grade.

"Are you Mrs. Hooper?"

The voice that called from outside the room sounded familiar. I held my breath.

"Yes," Mrs. Hooper answered.

Lacy Valentine strolled into the room, like she owned the place.

"I'm Lacy," she announced, loud enough so the whole room would hear. "I'm truly looking forward to being in your class."

I waved, but I guess Lacy didn't see me.

"Isn't this radical?" Brandy whispered behind my left ear. "Lacy and us in the same room. I mean, like we're going to be the most popular class in sixth grade."

CHAPTER

3

As Lacy "made her entrance," about six or seven other kids followed her into the room. Kids were always following Lacy. She was a real leader—someone everybody looked up to and wanted to be with. After Mrs. Hooper checked the group off her computer sheet and they sat down, about eight or nine more people drifted in. The seats in our class were almost full.

Mrs. Hooper was passing out the *Blyle Junior High Handbook* when I heard this cheerful voice say:

"Is this Mrs. Hooper's room?"

Everybody glanced toward the door. The face at the edge of the doorway was pretty. A short girl with big brown eyes and layered hair peeked in. She was so small, she looked more like a third grader than a sixth grader. Her eyes were wide, kind of like a little deer who had just been startled by a hunter or something—but at the same time, they had sort of a soft twinkle to them.

"My name's Judy Baird. Is this where I'm supposed to be?"

Mrs. Hooper scanned the computer sheet. "Judy Baird," she repeated, pointing at a name on her list. "You're in the right place."

The face at the doorway smiled. It was a warm and friendly smile. I remember thinking, "She's cute. Maybe Brandy and I will get her to join us for cheerleader practice at sixth hour."

She walked through the doorway, and the thought flew from my mind like fall leaves yanked from a tree in a blue norther. The little girl named Judy didn't walk into the room.

She dragged herself.

I'd never seen anyone stand sort of upright and drag herself, but that's exactly what she did. I saw the cane first. It was a long wooden stick with a crook on one end and a rubber tip on the other. As soon as it came through the door, the girl jerked her back and hips and dragged her right leg up beside it. She twisted and jerked to the other side to move her left leg up. She balanced there for a second, then put the cane out in front of her and did it again.

My eyes got wider and wider. Even though her walk looked awkward and horrible, she managed to make her way quite quickly across the room. She was almost halfway to Mrs. Hooper's desk before our teacher stopped her.

"Ah . . . er . . . Judy," she stammered, "why don't you take that desk right there by the door? It would . . . ah . . . make it easier on you to get in and out of the room."

Larry Don Perdue was already sitting in the first desk by the door. The look on his face was downright desperate, like he'd die if he didn't get to be the lookout. Mrs. Hooper pointed at him and snapped her fingers.

"Ah . . . Dave . . . no . . ." She traced a finger down the computer sheet.

"Larry Don," he sighed.

"Larry Don," she repeated, smiling. "Please move your things to that desk over by . . ."

Judy cleared her throat.

"It's really noisy by the door sometimes," she interrupted. "If it's all right, I'd just as soon sit over there." She gestured with the tip of her cane, then put it back on the floor to catch her balance. "If it's all right."

Mrs. Hooper shrugged.

"I guess."

Judy Baird dragged herself to the aisle next to mine. The whole room was quiet, even Mrs. Hooper, as the little girl maneuvered her way to the seat right across from me. With one hand holding tightly to her cane and the other clutching the front corner of the desk, she turned and practically fell into the chair. I didn't realize I was holding my breath until it whooshed out of me—relieved that she'd landed in the seat instead of on the floor.

Even after she was seated, we were quiet. I don't think anyone meant to stare, we just couldn't help it. Mrs. Hooper rattled the paper on her desk and coughed, and it was like the whole bunch of us suddenly realized what we were doing. We all jerked around to look at our teacher.

"Everybody is accounted for on my list but three students," Mrs. Hooper announced. "Does anyone know anything about a Beth Wheat, Justin Mincis, or a David Tanner?"

"David Tanner moved," a boy about two seats behind Larry Don answered. "He went to some little town in Oklahoma called Chichenshaw or Chickasaw or something like that. I don't think he's gonna be here."

Mrs. Hooper wrote something on her computer sheet.

"How about Beth Wheat or Justin Mincis?"

When no one answered, our teacher shrugged. She glanced at her watch and started passing out the handbooks again. "You have about thirty minutes left to read over your handbooks, and I'll try to answer any questions you have. We will also have a helper board. Each week I'll change names so a different person can run things to the office, clean erasers, and take names if I have to be out of the room. The last fifteen minutes of the school day, we will return to homeroom for announcements. Okay, go ahead and read over your handbooks."

I started reading. Every now and then, I peeked at the girl across the aisle from me. I didn't want her to see me looking at her. Then, as I glanced around the room, I noticed most of the others were sneaking peeks at her, just like I was.

"How horrible," I thought to myself. "I wonder what it would feel like to have people staring at you all the time?"

When the bell rang, Brandy and I made our way down the hall toward our next class. We stopped at our lockers—not that we had anything in there, we just wanted to see if we could open the dumb things. I turned mine left to 7, right to 26, then left to 11. Nothing happened. Brandy opened her locker on the first try. I twisted the little knob again.

"Courtney?" Lacy's voice startled me.

I went clear past 26 to 30, before I stopped to look up.

"Hi, Lacy."

She smiled back. "Check with your mom and see if you can come to my house Thursday after school. My mom will pick us up. We can work on the list and pick out some dance tapes or CDs."

"Okay." I nodded.

Brandy leaned toward us, trying to hear. "Party?" she whispered. I shushed her out of the corner of my mouth.

"I think we should invite most of the people in our homeroom and then . . ." Frowning, Lacy paused for a second. "Oh, do either of you know that little crippled girl who came in?" She put a hand to her mouth, barely touching her lips with the tips of her fingers. "Whoops, maybe I should say handicapped, instead of crippled."

I nodded my agreement. "I think you're right, Lacy. That is a better term than crippled."

Next to me, Brandy cleared her throat.

"Like, both of you are totally out of touch. The current, politically correct expression is 'physically challenged.'"

"The best word is Judy." A soft, pleasant voice made all three of us stop and spin around. Judy Baird was right behind us. She didn't stop or even look in our direction when she added: "But if Judy is too hard for you to remember, crippled or handicapped is fine. It doesn't matter."

There was no anger or bitterness in her voice. She simply dragged herself past us and shuffled down the hall.

I felt my face get all hot. None of us had realized she'd been so near—close enough to hear us talking about her. I'd never felt so embarrassed.

As I watched her struggle through the crowded hall—as I saw all the people staring at her and whispering—the shame was chased away by a strange feeling in the pit of my stomach.

Poor thing. She must feel all those eyes on her. How pitiful.

CHAPTER

4

Daddy and I changed out the carburetor after supper. It was nine o'clock before we finished. He didn't say much about his talk with Coach Bentley. All he mentioned was that Ben would be starting quarterback for the high-school football team and that Coach Bentley was a little concerned about one of the guys Ben was running around with.

That night, when I went to bed, I couldn't keep from thinking about the little crippled girl who took the desk next to me in homeroom. Her face was so pretty, but the way she walked was so pitiful.

After two days, I wasn't quite sure whether or not "pitiful" was the right word for Judy Baird.

It seemed like everybody watched her for the

first couple of days. We watched her drag her legs behind her cane. We watched her carry her books down the hall from one class to the next. We watched her sit down in a chair and were amazed each time she landed in the thing instead of on the floor. And we watched her carry her tray across the lunchroom. Even though some of the boys offered to help her with it, she politely refused. She somehow always managed to make it to her seat without spilling anything.

Lunch seemed to give her the most problems. Not really lunch, it was the recess we had afterward. In grade school we got a morning, noon, and afternoon recess. In junior high we only got a thirty-minute break after lunch.

The sixth grade and half of the seventh had first lunch. The seventh graders always got the tables near the door and the windows. That left us sixth graders who used to go to West with the tables by the serving line and in the middle of the room. Not even Lacy was cool enough to get to sit with the seventh graders, but she did get the table right next to them in the center of the cafeteria. Lacy asked me and about ten of her best friends to sit at the big round table with her. Brandy didn't make it, but she told me it was all right and she got the table right next to us. Kids who used to go to Bedford

Elementary got the places between us and the kids from Kennedy, who had to take the tables near the tray dump and the garbage. It was noisy there, and sometimes when the air conditioner wasn't working too well, it kind of smelled.

It was funny the way everybody seemed to stay with kids from their old school and how we staked out tables in the lunchroom—the kids from West school near the seventh graders, the Bedford kids in the middle, and the Kennedy kids clear over by the trash.

When we finished lunch and went out on the school grounds, most everybody still had their "proper" places. The seventh-grade boys either played softball on the east field or basketball on the courts closest to the building. The girls sat on the steps or stood around and visited in the shade near the lunchroom annex. The sixth-grade boys were all over the place. They either played softball on the west field or basketball on the "far" court (the basket there wasn't as good as the others and the concrete was cracked), or they played football between the softball fields or just ran around wrestling, scuffling, or clunking each other on the head like doofy boys normally do.

Lacy and the rest of us from West sat on the parallel bars next to the basketball court. There were three sets of bars, and we got the ones closest to the basketball court and the seventh-grade boys. From there we could either watch the boys, or if no cute guys were playing, we could watch Theresa Dayton. In second grade, Theresa decided she wanted to grow up to be a twirler in the high-school band. Her mom got her a silver baton with white rubber tips on both ends. She'd been practicing ever since. Theresa dropped the thing a lot, and when she threw it up in the air, she never caught it. Right before it came down, she'd scream and run out of the way. It was funny.

The girls from Bedford sat on the steps by the sixth-grade entrance or played in the shade next to the windows. That left the girls from Kennedy without any place to hang around, so they just kind of wandered.

The wandering around is what bothered the little crippled girl. There was a steep hill between the lunchroom and the basketball courts. Sometimes, Judy would get going too fast when she came out of the lunchroom and fall down the steep slope. It was horrible to watch. She'd just kind of tip forward and sprawl on the ground. If any of the boys were running around near her, sometimes one would stop and help her get up. Usually, one of us girls would jump off the parallel bars to go help. But most of the time she got up by herself.

Watching Judy get up wasn't a pretty sight either. She'd sit up and put her cane beside her with the rubber tip on the ground and the crook behind her right shoulder. With her thumbs near the rubber tip, she'd turn and start walking her hands up the shaft. When her hands were almost at the top, she'd pull herself up, her feet in front and the cane still behind, helping her to balance. She'd lean forward, and just before she tipped over on her face, she'd whip the cane in front of her and catch her balance. It was a tricky process, but I was amazed how fast she could do it and take off again.

I think the thing that really bothered me was the black girl named La Shea. I guess she and Judy were friends because La Shea sat in the desk right in front of Judy in homeroom and they were always talking. They ate together in the lunchroom and wandered around the playground together, too.

But La Shea sure didn't act like a friend. She was almost always with Judy on the grounds, but not once did La Shea ever offer to help her up when she fell. La Shea just stood there, looking off toward where they had been headed, and waited for someone to help Judy or for her to get up all by herself.

It just didn't seem right.

I felt sorry for Judy. I guess that's how you're supposed to feel around handicapped people. But she was nice and she seemed to have lots of other friends besides La Shea—so maybe pitiful wasn't the right word. After the first couple of days, we quit staring at her so much and busied ourselves with important things—things like trying to find where our classes were, trying to figure out who to visit with, stopping by our locker, or going to the bathroom and still making it to our next class before the tardy bell rang, and . . . Lacy's party.

Brandy never could keep a secret. By noon on the first day of school, practically everyone in the sixth grade knew that Lacy had asked me to help plan her party. By the second day of school, people I didn't even know were coming up to me and introducing themselves. All the attention was fun.

CHAPTER

5

"Judy went to Kennedy Elementary last year. She lives in what they call No Hope Village and the reason she's like she is is because she's got cerebral palsy." I stopped talking about Judy Baird just long enough to take a drink of my iced tea.

Daddy had finished his supper and was reading the evening paper. He peeked over the top of it when I stopped talking.

"Amy Diggs, this girl in my science class who went to Kennedy last year," I continued, "Amy says that most everybody liked her, only she never had a best friend. That's on account of her mother. Amy says everybody at No Hope Village thinks Judy's mom is some kind of witch or something. She's always griping at people and telling them to leave her daughter alone. They say she's real mean, too. She yells at Judy to do her chores and if Judy falls down, her mom makes her get up all by herself. She won't let anyone help her."

I took another sip of tea. The glass was wet, and the cold water that dripped off it and onto my leg made me jump.

"When Amy explained about Judy's mother, I figured that's why La Shea never helps her—she's scared of the old witch. Judy really seems sweet, though. She's got this great laugh. I kind of like her. You think I should ask Lacy about inviting her to the party? Or maybe I could have her over some evening first and . . ."

"People like that are best left alone," Emily said, dabbing the corner of her mouth with a napkin. "Not that I have anything against cripples, you understand. It's not that at all. But the fact that she went to Kennedy and lives in No Hope Village . . . surely you can find someone better to spend time with."

"What's wrong with people from No Hope Village, anyway?" I asked. "I mean, I've heard of it, but what is it?"

Daddy glanced up from his newspaper. "It's an apartment complex down on Forty-ninth Street—down in the Ryland Heights area. Low-rent housing. It's really named New Hope Village but people stuck the name No Hope on it. Lots of people on welfare, and the government subsidizes their rent and . . ."

"Low rent, indeed," Emily interrupted. "No Hope Village is the dregs of humanity. It's a pit. There's nothing down there but drug dealers and thieves."

"Now, Emily," Daddy soothed, "that's not quite right. There's some good, decent people who live there, folks just sort of down on their luck. José Ormondo lived there awhile, before I hired him. He's a good worker. Now that he has a job, he has his own apartment over on . . ."

"José Ormondo," Emily growled. "Just my point. Nothing down there but Hispanics, blacks, and Orientals. Immigrants. They're lazy and . . ."

"But Judy's white," I interrupted.

Emily sneered.

"Well, if her mother lives in No Hope Village, with all those trashy people, she's nothing but poor white trash."

Ben was sitting across from me at the table. He shoved his plate so hard, it clinked against his tea glass and almost knocked it over. He rocked back on two legs of his chair.

"You're the authority on poor white trash, right, Emily?"

A little ripple of nausea rumbled through my stomach. Emily glared at Ben like he was a bug she wanted to squash. A blue vein popped out on her temple. Ben rocked back farther in his chair. Emily yanked the napkin from her lap and threw it down so hard on her plate, the silverware bounced and jingled. She leaped to her feet like she was going to reach across the table and hit my brother. Daddy yanked the newspaper from in front of his face and crunched it in his lap.

"Ben!" he roared. "I wish we could sit down to supper without . . ."

"Well, she started it," Ben snapped back. "Always talking about blacks and Hispanics. Always trying to put somebody down. Dexter's my best friend. Can't even have him over to our house 'cause he's black. That's the only way Emily can feel better about herself—putting somebody else down. Just once . . ."

"That's enough, Ben!"

The little ripple of nausea that raced through my stomach was fast turning into a full-blown knot. It went from my stomach clear up into my throat. Emily leaned toward my brother. The vein on her temple was bigger and bluer than before. Then, she glanced at Daddy. It was almost like she forced herself to calm down. The vein got smaller. Her bottom lip pouched out and she made a loud sniffling sound. Ben just looked at her. Emily yanked her plate from the table and sniffled louder.

"I don't have to listen to this smart-mouth," she said, almost whimpering. "Your father and I do everything we can to give you the things you need. Work and slave. This is the thanks we get." Still whimpering like she was about to cry, she put the dishes in the sink. "My parents never had much. I grew up poor, but I've brought myself up by my bootstraps to make a better life for myself. It's been a hard climb, but . . ."

"Hard climb is right," Ben muttered under his breath. "How many husbands have you climbed over to . . ."

"Ben!" Daddy leaped to his feet. When he did, his chair went clattering across the kitchen linoleum. "That's enough! Go to your room, *right now!!!*"

Ben banged his chair down on all four legs. For an instant, he looked at Daddy. Then, shaking his head, he got up and went to his room. After a time, Daddy sat back down and began uncrumpling his newspaper. His hands shook, and he kept shooting blasts of hair up his forehead. They made the little wisp of hair on the top of his head bounce. Emily started on the dishes, still mumbling to herself about how ungrateful Ben was and how hard she worked to finish real-estate school in Dallas and how hard her job was at the Parker Realty Company.

I just sat there, shaking all over and hoping the

knot in my stomach wouldn't make me throw up my supper. I hated fights. I hated it when people yelled or said bad things to one another. And lately at home, it seemed like there were more and more fights. Somehow, I made my legs stop trembling long enough so I could get up from my chair. I carried the rest of the dishes to the sink. I didn't want to help Emily with the dishes. I didn't want to be around anyone. All I wanted to do was run to my room and hide under my bed. I just wanted to get away from the fighting and the yelling and the way it made me feel inside.

The phone rang, and it was the most beautiful sound I ever heard.

It broke the sound of Emily's muttering and Daddy's and my silence. It rang a second time, but not a third.

"Courtney? For you," Ben called from down the hall.

It was my chance to escape. I put the towel beside the sink, promised Emily I'd dry the dishes later, and bolted down the hall to the safety of my room. It didn't matter who was on the phone. I didn't care. All I thought about was getting away from the anger in the kitchen, an anger that hung in the air so hot and sticky, it was like a big dog breathing on me.

CHAPTER

6

I was glad Lacy had called last night to remind me to ask about going to her house tomorrow. For one thing, it got me away from all the anger in the kitchen. For another, with all the fighting, I might have forgotten to even ask, if Lacy hadn't called.

Thursday seemed to drag by as slowly as a snail crawling up a high wall. Classes were boring and the only excitement at lunch recess was when Theresa threw her baton and it hit one of the seventh-grade boys. We all thought he was going to beat her over the head with the thing. When he picked up the baton and started toward her, Theresa let out a little squeal and took off for the school building. The boy just shook his head, handed the baton to one of the girls on the parallel bars, and went back to his basketball game.

All afternoon, I waited for the bell. It seemed like forever before it finally rang.

Lacy met me at the lockers and we walked out to find her mom. We spotted the blue Dodge minivan. Lacy's mom was leaning out the window, visiting with Jessica Tusami's mom. We hopped in and put our seat belts on.

Mrs. Valentine was a tall, slender woman. She was easy to talk with, too. As soon as Mrs. Tusami left and we headed out of the parking lot, she started visiting with me. We talked all the way to Lacy's house.

The first thing I noticed when we stopped in the driveway was how big the Valentines' home was. It was a huge, two-story brick house with a steep roof. We could have put our whole house inside the second floor and it wouldn't have filled it up.

The second thing I noticed was the flowers. The enormous yard that surrounded the home was filled with all colors of cannas. There were rosebushes and lilacs, and right as we went through the front door, I noticed the smell of honeysuckle. I paused a moment and looked around. A long, beautifully trimmed hedge ran from the front porch to the corner of the house.

"Come on in," Mrs. Valentine urged as she opened the door wider.

"Sorry." I smiled. "I just noticed the honey-suckle."

"They're my favorite," she said.

"Mine, too."

Already, I could tell that I loved Mrs. Valentine. She liked flowers, especially honeysuckle. She was tall and pretty. She was probably just like my mom would be if she were still . . .

"Come on, Courtney," Lacy called from the stair-case in front of me, "my room's up here."

Lacy's room was gorgeous. Everything was trimmed in pink. She had pink curtains with lace ruffles. There was a pink bedspread on her queen-size water bed and pink lace shams on the pillows. On the mirrored dresser at the far wall was a vase filled with fresh-cut pink roses.

"What do you think?" Lacy swept her arm around the room.

I shrugged.

"Pink."

Instantly, I clamped a hand over my mouth. I couldn't believe I'd said that. I mean, why not some-thing like, "Oh, it's a beautiful room," or "How lovely," or "Simply gorgeous"? No—all I could think to say was—"Pink." What a dumb, klutzy thing to say.

"No kidding." Lacy just laughed. "Don't feel embarrassed. It *is* pink. Mother's had this thing for pink ever since I was born. It's enough to make me puke."

She motioned me to her closet. I stood beside her as she dug around a moment and pulled something out. She held up a black, see-through blouse. Stuffing that under her arm, she held up a pair of black, see-through bell-bottoms.

"Think I should wear these to the party?"

I blinked. I guess my eyes were so wide, they almost popped out of my head. I blinked again.

"I could never . . ." I gasped.

Lacy laughed.

"It's not really that bad." She dug in her closet again and pulled out a hanger. Proudly, Lacy held up what looked like a bikini bathing suit. There was a tiny black top and a pair of low-cut black bottoms. "The thing's not really see-through. You wear this under it."

She laid the outfit on her bed. "Want to try it on? My brother lives in Montebello, California. He found this radical little shop called Cool Jerk. It's the in place for retro fashions. It's really neat."

I frowned, staring at the weird outfit on her bed.

"What's retro fashions?"

"You know," she answered, "styles from the sixties and seventies. Stuff like that's really popular, what with old TV things like 'The Brady Bunch' and

'The Partridge Family' making a big comeback. Anyway, when Tony calls and asks what I want for Christmas or my birthday, I tell him anything that's in and sexy, and *not* pink. Wouldn't the boys just flip if I wore this?"

I twisted a strand of blond hair around my finger. "I could never . . ."

"Oh, quit being such a prude," Lacy scoffed. "Besides," she shrugged and hung the things back in her closet, "my mom would never let me wear it. At least it's not pink."

We went downstairs and got some CDs. Lacy opened up a big cabinet and put about five of the CDs in a machine. Then she flipped a couple of switches.

"This will turn on the speakers by the pool," she said. "Let's go out there and make a list of who we're going to invite."

We didn't put many people on the list. Mostly, we talked and listened to the music. We laughed and visited about boys and giggled about how dumb the soap operas were and all sorts of things. At four-thirty, we ran up to Lacy's room to watch "Wavelength" on her TV, then we worked on the list again. We were still working on it when it was time for Mrs. Valentine to take me home, so Lacy went with us.

"I just don't know," Lacy said from the backseat.

"Judy seems sweet, but I'm just afraid she'd feel out of place."

"Why?" I asked.

Lacy shrugged. "Well, being handicapped and all. We're going to have dancing and be out by the pool in our bathing suits. It might make her feel uncomfortable."

"She doesn't have to wear a bathing suit, if she doesn't want to." I pushed my tongue against the side of my cheek. "You could be right about the dancing, though. Judy might really feel out of place or ashamed or . . . you know . . . something like that."

"Who are you two talking about?" Mrs. Valentine asked.

We explained about Judy Baird, and how we both liked her but didn't know if we should invite her to the party or not. Finally, Mrs. Valentine helped us out.

"I think you should ask her. If she feels self-conscious, she doesn't have to dance or wear a bathing suit, or even come to the party for that matter, but I think the best thing would be to invite her and let her make the decision about how she feels."

Mrs. Valentine pulled into our driveway, and I hopped out. As she and Lacy drove away, I wondered if she used Vel soap.

The thought brought a smile to my face. But as I

turned to go into the house, my shoulders sagged. I hoped Ben and Emily weren't inside fighting. I reached for the doorknob, but hated to go in. I wished they'd just leave each other alone.

My wish came true. Ben and Emily ate supper without so much as one cross word. When we finished, Ben went to his room and started his homework. Daddy and I did the dishes. A little peace and quiet was a nice change. Trouble was, it didn't last.

Friday morning, Judy, La Shea, and I were trying to finish up our math homework before Mrs. Hooper came in to start English. Greg and Joshua were scampering around the room. They were always up, doing something, before our teacher came in. All Brandy wanted to do was talk about the party.

Brandy leaned back in her chair. "Like, did you ask Lacy if I could come to the party?"

It was almost as if Brandy had tunnel vision or something. The party was all she ever thought about.

"Yes." I nodded and shushed her.

"How about the other girls at my lunch table? Any luck getting them invited?"

"I'm trying to finish my math," I snapped. "You already finished?"

"No, but it's easy. I'll do it between classes."

"I can't get the bonus problem," I heard Judy whisper to La Shea. "It says, 'Fill in the missing numbers to complete the sequence, 1, 3, 5, —, —, 13.'"

"Rebecca Simer is another one who . . ." Brandy stopped right in the middle of her sentence and glanced at Judy. "Seven and eleven go in the blanks," she said.

"Huh?" Judy frowned.

"They're primes."

Judy tilted her head. "What's that?"

"Primes or primary numbers are numbers that can only be divided by themselves and one. Seven and eleven are the two that are missing in the sequence. After thirteen comes seventeen, then . . ."

"We haven't even studied that stuff," La Shea protested.

Brandy shrugged. "That's why it's a bonus problem." Then, like she had never stopped talking to me while she solved the math problem that had the three of us stuck, she went right on: "Along with Rebecca Simer, Sonya Martin will just die if she doesn't get invited and . . ."

"Joshua! Stop it! Give that back!"

The loud shout made me jump. I glanced at Judy. She leaned to the side and almost turned over her chair.

"Joshua, give it back! NOW!!!"

Joshua trotted up the aisle. He had Judy's cane. About halfway to the front of the room, he stopped and turned back to her. He held the cane out, dangling it like a doggy treat for a puppy to jump at.

"You want it, come and get it."

"I mean it, Joshua," Judy growled, struggling from her seat. "Bring it back."

Balancing, she held the backs of chairs and desks as she went up the aisle toward him. Suddenly, one of the desks she was leaning against tipped. Judy and the desk toppled to the floor.

Joshua looked surprised. For a moment, I thought he was going to come back, give Judy her cane, and help her up. He took a step toward her and stopped.

"Cool move," he chuckled. "Now, can you roll over and play dead?"

A boy named Bobby Bozworth sat at the back on the far side of the room. As Joshua jiggled the cane, taunting Judy with it, Bobby slowly walked over and helped Judy to her feet. He asked if she was all right, then practically carried her back to her chair.

"I'll go get your cane," he said softly.

Judy rubbed at her knee. I guess she'd hit the floor pretty hard. Suddenly, I noticed the little twinkle in her eye.

"Wait." She glanced at Joshua, then turned and looked back at his empty chair. Finally, she smiled up at Bobby. "Just keep him busy for a minute. Chase him or something. I got an idea."

While Bobby started up the aisle toward Joshua, Judy leaned down and got her lunch box. Joshua ran to Mrs. Hooper's desk and Bobby followed him. Judy took something from the lunch box, but I was so busy watching Bobby and Joshua, I didn't see what it was. Bobby flushed Joshua from behind the teacher's desk. Still holding the cane, Joshua made it to the doorway. I heard the crinkle of cellophane, but again I was so busy watching the boys, I couldn't tell what Judy had unwrapped. Joshua darted out the door with Bobby hot on his heels.

The second they were gone, Judy shoved herself up from her chair. She carried something in her right hand and used her left to balance herself as she walked back to Joshua's empty chair. With Becky Keats and Kenneth Loffler in the way, between me and Joshua's desk, I couldn't see what she put on Joshua's chair. Kenneth started laughing, but when Larry Don called from the front of the room, "Hooper's coming," Kenneth slapped a hand over his mouth and turned to face the front.

Bobby darted through the doorway. "Teacher's coming!" He echoed Larry Don's warning as he ran for his chair. Judy, leaning on the desks, dragged herself back to her seat. She fell into it just as Joshua slid through the doorway. He ran down the aisle, dropped the cane beside Judy, and practically dived into his chair.

There was rustling and a lot of scurrying around. By the time Mrs. Hooper walked in, we were all facing the front of the room as quiet as mice. Our teacher folded her arms and glared out at us.

"What's going on?" she demanded. "Joshua, I saw you out in the hall."

We turned to see what he was going to say.

"I wasn't doin' nothin'," he lied. "I just had to go get a drink and . . ."

The weirdest look suddenly swept across Joshua's face. His nose crinkled up and he kind of wiggled his seat. Then his nose crinkled some more. In slow motion, he eased from his chair. He stood and tried to look behind him—first one direction, then the other. When he couldn't see his butt, he reached back. As he brought his hand around, I saw a glob of white, sticky, mushy stuff mixed with yellow crumbs stuck to his skin.

"Twinkies?!?!?" Joshua gasped. Then he looked at Mrs. Hooper. "I got to go to the bathroom."

He waddled across the room, walking with his legs kind of apart, like some little kid who'd messed in his diapers. The whole class burst out laughing. Kenneth fell out of his chair. Molly Pierce jumped up with her legs crossed. "I have to go to the bathroom," she giggled, then took off for the door.

As Joshua walked, little globs of smushed Twinkies dropped from the seat of his pants, leaving a trail across the classroom. Everyone was in stitches.

"All right," Mrs. Hooper yelled when Joshua paused at the doorway, "who put the Twinkies in his chair?"

Everyone laughed again. Then, as if on some unseen signal, every single one of us ducked our heads into our books and acted like we were working.

Joshua stood at the door for a moment. He glared at Judy. It wasn't really a glare—it was worse—I couldn't quite describe the expression on his face, only, it was the meanest, most hateful look I'd ever seen.

Judy only smiled at him.

It was funny, but the look on Joshua's face made a knot kind of kink up in the pit of my stomach. "This is all I need," I thought to myself as I watched Joshua waddle out of the room. "Got Ben and Emily settled down at home. Now I'm in the middle between Judy and Joshua at school. Why can't people just leave each other alone?"

CHAPTER

7

"Why can't people just leave each other alone?"

For a second, I thought I heard an echo. I remembered asking myself that in Mrs. Hooper's homeroom. Now Ben was sitting in the front seat of his car, asking the exact same question.

On Friday afternoons, if Ben had a home football game, he picked me up after school instead of me having to ride the bus. I hated riding the bus. The noise was enough to cross my eyes, and somebody was always scuffling or hitting someone else or throwing junk. The bus was Emily's idea. Lately she'd been having to work late with Mr. Parker at his realty company in Dallas and couldn't pick me up. Daddy didn't close his auto shop until five, and most afternoons, Ben was at football practice. There was no football practice on Fridays, though, which was why he could pick me up. His friend Dexter was usually with him, and Ben would drop him at his house on our way home.

We had to drive through the Ryland Heights area of town. Since No Hope Village was right in the middle of the Ryland Heights area, Emily said the same things about both places—"Nothing there but drug dealers and thieves." From the car, I could tell that the houses here weren't very nice. There were a lot of bars along the main streets and scuzzy-looking men sort of hung around in front of them. Maybe Emily was right.

Ben jerked the car to a sudden stop, jarring me from my thoughts. I braced my hand against the back of the seat to keep from flying forward. A little, white-haired woman shuffled in front of us, making her way across the road. Dexter glanced back at me from the front seat.

"You okay, General George?"

I smiled and nodded. As long as I could remember, Dexter had called me General George—it was really short for General George Armstrong Custer, a Civil War general and Indian fighter who had long blond hair like mine. I kind of liked the nickname. It was better than being called "squirt" or "shorty" or something like that. I liked Dexter, too. He had happy eyes. I don't really know how to describe them. They were just happy. There were little wrinkles at the corners, wrinkles that went up instead of down, I guess because he smiled a lot.

Ben thumped the steering wheel with his palm, trying to hurry the old lady across the road.

"I'm not naive enough to think that everybody's gonna love each other or get along all the time," Ben started talking to Dexter again. "But why do they have to fight? I mean, if they don't like each other, fine! Why can't they just leave each other alone?"

"It doesn't work like that." Dexter shrugged. "You live down here, you either belong or you're out in the cold. Simple as that."

"Bull!" Ben snapped. "You live here. You've never been in a gang or done stuff like that."

Dexter ran his huge hand through his short, curly hair.

"I don't live down here, Ben. We're more on the edge. Ronald and Donald live right in the heart of Ryland Heights. Besides, you know my dad. You know what he'd do if I so much as got in a car with those guys. Shoot, I went to the shoe store last winter and got me a pair of black, high-top Gear's. When my dad saw them, he pitched 'em in the trash 'cause he said that's what all the 'Reds' down in Flatwood were wearing. It was part of their 'colors.' "

I had no idea what Ben and Dexter were talking about. It was almost like they were speaking in some sort of code or something. I did figure out that they were talking about gangs that ran around in this area and some guy named Ronald, who we were going to pick up before we took Dexter home. Other than that . . .

"I still think Ronald could make it," Ben said. "I don't really think he's doing drugs or running with the gangs, yet. He's got speed and good hands. He's not nearly as good a wide receiver as you are, but if we can keep him in football, maybe he's got a chance."

"I don't know." Dexter sighed. "His twin brother is definitely in. Donald talks the talk and wears the colors and . . ."

"Donald's a jerk. He was a jerk even back in junior high," Ben interrupted. "That doesn't mean that Ronald . . ."

Suddenly, Ben jammed on his brakes again. The tires even squealed. This time, I wasn't quick enough to get my hand braced against the back of the seat. My shoulder whacked into the u

"You see that?" Ben yelped.

"All I saw was the dash and the windsh ... com
ing at my head," Dexter answered, pushing himself
back into the seat.

"Over there," Ben pointed. "That kid just
knocked that little girl down. Just shoved her flat on
her face."

Dexter and I looked where Ben was pointing. I
saw a girl in a blue dress lying on the ground. A boy
stood above her, shaking his finger and yelling.

My eyes flashed. The boy was Joshua. The little
girl sat up. It was Judy Baird.

She twisted around and put her cane beside her
with the rubber tip on the ground and the crook
behind her right arm. With her thumbs near the
tip, she started walking her hands up—lifting her
bottom from the ground. When she was about halfway up, Joshua reached out with his foot and slid
the tip of the cane out from under her. Judy landed
on her bottom with a thud.

"Gawh!" Ben growled. "You see that? Poor little thing, trying to get up on her cane and he . . .
I'm . . . I'm gonna go beat the crap out of that
little . . ."

The door handle clicked, but before Ben could
leap out of the car, Dexter caught his arm.

"Wait."

Ben tried to jerk free.

"What do ya mean, wait? Didn't you see what the little punk did to her?"

"Just hold on," Dexter soothed. "I know that kid. Her name's Judy. She'll handle him. Just hold on."

Ben, still jerking against Dexter's grip, let go of the door and turned to watch. I jumped up on my knees and practically climbed on top of Dexter's shoulders so I could see better.

Judy put the tip of her cane on the ground and started working her hands up it once more. But this time, when Joshua moved toward her, she let go and plopped to the ground by herself.

It all happened so quickly, it was almost a blur. Judy let go of her cane, flipped it so she had hold of the crook, and hit Joshua across the shin with the shaft. I could hear the POP even from where we sat—almost a half block away.

Like I said, it was quick. One second, Judy was sitting on the ground, the next, she was on her feet and Joshua was yelling and hopping around, holding his leg.

Once Judy had her balance, she raised her cane again. She brought it down across Joshua's back. I could hear the loud WHACK sound.

Joshua screamed and took off.

We watched him running and hollering down the

street. If he'd been lying down, it would have looked like he was doing sit-ups or something. He'd run a little ways, then lean down to rub his shin. A couple of steps later, he'd arch his back, trying to reach the stinging spot between his shoulder blades with his hand. Bend over, arch back, bend over, arch back—every two steps or so, while he was running.

"What'd I tell ya?" Dexter jabbed Ben with his elbow and laughed. "Said she'd handle him, didn't I?"

Ben laughed, too. "Man, watch that kid go. You'd think she was hot on his heels, the way he's sprinting. He's moving faster than you do on a wide-out pass pattern."

They both laughed. I didn't. I smiled, though. It was a big smile that stretched the corners of my mouth.

A car honked behind us. Ben pulled around the corner and parked at the curb. I guess he wanted to make sure that Judy got home without Joshua coming back to pester her again. Judy dragged her legs behind her cane and quickly made her way across the street. There was a big apartment complex there—six three-story buildings that all looked the same. The buildings were sort of a gray color and needed paint. Some of the screens dangled loose from the windows. Judy made her way to the building on the end. When she stepped onto the porch, the screen door swung open for her. She disappeared inside. I wished Ben had pulled the car up a little farther because I just knew it was her mother who opened the door. I was eager to catch a glimpse of The Witch of No Hope Village.

Once Ben was sure Judy was safe in her apartment, he drove on. "One tough little kid," he chuckled. "She's as quick with that cane as a rattlesnake striking at a mouse."

Dexter rocked back in the seat. "She's a sweet kid," he said. "But you're right, she's tough as a boot."

We drove about two blocks to another bunch of apartments. These were smaller than the ones where Judy lived. When Ben honked the horn, a black boy came trotting out. Dexter swung the door open and scooted over next to Ben. Their sport bags were piled next to me in the backseat. I kind of leaned to the side so the kid who came running out could throw his bag back here, too. Only, he didn't. He sat next to Dexter and clutched the bag in his lap like the equipment inside was a valuable treasure or something.

"Ronald," Ben glanced back at me, "this is my kid sister, Courtney."

Ronald looked at me. He didn't say anything, he

just sort of grunted. I didn't much care for Ronald. He looked mean and sour, sort of like someone who'd been sucking on lemons or something. I sat quietly as we drove to Dexter's house and let out both boys.

"See you about a quarter of six," Ben called as we drove away. "Want to sit up here, kid?"

I climbed over the seat and plopped down next to my brother. We didn't say much as we drove home. I kept smiling, though. I couldn't get the picture of Judy whacking Joshua with her cane out of my mind. I was glad she'd taken care of him. Judging by the way he ran for home, I was pretty sure that he wouldn't bother Judy Baird again. The fight that started at school between them was over. Now, if there was only some way I could keep Ben and Emily from fussing at one another . . .

"Ben? How come you don't like Emily?"

I wished I'd kept my big mouth shut.

CHAPTER

8

Ben was still smiling. I guess, like me, he was thinking about how Judy had handled herself when Joshua tried to beat her up on the way home from school. But the second I said the word "Emily," the corners of his mouth drooped toward the floorboard and his eyes got real tight.

He hesitated for a long time. He didn't look at me.

"She's no good," he said finally.

"I didn't like her at first either," I confessed. "But I kinda like her now."

"Yeah, right." Ben coughed. "You're falling for her stuff, too. She buys you new clothes, takes you to the beauty shop once a week. That costs a bundle. You think money grows on trees?"

"Emily's not all that bad, Ben. Besides, Daddy's happy when he's with her and . . ."

"Yeah," Ben snapped, glaring straight ahead at the road, "she makes him happy, but she's gonna end up breaking his heart, 'cause she's no good."

I folded my arms and glared at him.

"Why do you keep saying, 'She's no good'? What do you mean?"

"Emily's just using him."

"Huh?"

"She found out he owned the auto shop and figured that was a good meal ticket. You know he had to take a loan out on the place. Between all the clothes she buys, the dues she pays to those hotshot clubs she keeps joining, and the cost of getting her through that dumb real-estate school, he's already behind on his payments to the bank. If business doesn't pick up, he's likely to lose the shop. Now that the cash is running out, you just watch. She'll dump Dad and take up with some other guy. She's already been married three times. Just watch."

I shook my head.

"Her last husband was mean to her. He hit her and stuff like that. I heard her tell Daddy about it once. I don't blame her for leaving somebody like that."

"Yeah." Ben made a snorting noise. "That's her story."

"And now that she's finished school and got a job at the real-estate place, she's making money."

Ben shot me an angry glance. "Yeah, and you see her closet? New outfits, so she can look nice when she goes to work. New shoes. She hasn't helped Dad a bit when it comes to paying the bank."

"But Daddy loves her. He loved Mama. He wouldn't love somebody if they weren't any good, would he? Besides, he's happy." I brushed a strand of blond hair from the corner of my mouth. "Remember how we used to catch him crying sometimes after Mama died? He never laughed. He just worked and sat in front of the TV and he never went anyplace. When he met Emily . . . well, it's the first time since Mama died that he's really been happy."

"He's happy because . . ."

Ben stopped right in the middle of his sentence. He looked over at me with his mouth open.

"What?" I asked.

When he shut his mouth, it made kind of a popping sound. Frowning, he studied me a moment, then shook his head and looked back at the road.

"What?" I repeated.

"Nothing."

"What?"

Ben's chest sort of caved in when he sighed. He looked over, studying me again. His cheek bulged out where his tongue traced tiny circles inside his mouth.

"Well," he said, clearing his throat, "for an old lady, she isn't bad to look at. Her face is okay, and she's built pretty good for somebody her age. She probably wiggled and flipped around and . . . and . . . ah . . . well, Dad's a man . . . and . . ." He looked at me again and shook his head. "Never mind."

He turned back to his driving, locking his hands on the steering wheel and his eyes on the road. I folded my arms and watched the road, too.

I knew Ben wouldn't talk to me anymore about it. He still treated me like a little kid, like I hadn't had human growth and development last year in fifth grade and like I didn't know anything. But he was wrong about Daddy. Daddy wouldn't fall for somebody just because she was sexy. Daddy was smarter than that. He was better. Daddy was . . . well, Daddy was my daddy.

We got to sit in the box seats at the football game that night. Emily didn't make it. She called Daddy at the shop and said she had to work late to close a house sale that she and Mr. Parker had been working on. Since Ben was the starting quarterback, Daddy and I got to sit in the box seats right on the fifty-yard line. Mr. and Mrs. Langley, Dexter's mom and dad, sat with us. It was neat. Mrs. Langley kept getting excited. She'd yell and jump up and down and wave this handkerchief in big circles around her head every time Ben threw Dexter a pass. As I watched her, I knew where Dexter got his happy eyes. She was cute. Mr. Langley and Daddy visited about cars and stuff. When Ben and Dexter would make a good play, they'd cheer and high-five and brag on their sons to the people sitting in the seats next to us.

We beat Bellmont High by two touchdowns. Ben played a great game.

After the game Ben stayed with the rest of the team to listen to the coach. Then a bunch of the guys went cruising in their cars or met down at the Sonic or one of the drive-ins to get something to eat. Daddy and I went on home.

Emily was waiting for us when we got in. She was sitting in Daddy's recliner in her baggy, pink bathrobe and her fuzzy, pink slippers. She'd washed all her makeup off and had her hair in curlers.

"We beat Bellmont twenty-one to seven," Daddy boasted. Then, noticing the pillow she had clutched to her stomach, he frowned. "You all right?"

Emily pouted.

"Jim and I took the Davidsons to this fancy restaurant to close the sale on their house. I can't tell whether I drank too much or ate too much or both." She hugged the pillow harder. "I feel rotten."

"I'm sorry, hon," Daddy soothed, walking toward her. "Is there anything I can get for you?"

Emily rocked forward.

"Courtney, you're supposed to call Lacy."

I glanced at the clock on the mantel. "It's eleven."

"That's okay." She moaned and wrapped herself more tightly around the pillow. "They just got home from the football game, too. She wants to talk to you about your list of people for the party next weekend."

I trotted toward the phone in the hall. For a second, I glanced back. Daddy knelt beside Emily. He felt her forehead to see if she had any temperature. Then, he kissed her on the cheek.

Emily burped and hugged her pillow.

Ben was wrong. If he could see them right now— Emily with no makeup and sitting there in her sloppy, pink robe and slippers and Daddy on his knee . . . well . . . Ben was wrong. I didn't know what guys thought was pretty or sexy. I did know that, right now, Emily *wasn't it*. Daddy and Emily really loved each other. My daddy couldn't love her if she was no good.

A smile came to my face.

CHAPTER

9

The whole next week I just kept right on smiling. Every day after school, Mrs. Valentine drove Lacy and me over to her house to prepare for the big party. On Wednesday, Emily didn't have to work, so Mrs. Valentine asked her and a couple of other women from her club to come and help with the party, too.

Mrs. Carter and Mrs. Sikes had to leave early. While Lacy and I finished writing names on the invitations and put them in the envelopes, we could hear Emily and Mrs. Valentine talking and laughing downstairs. It sounded like they were having even more fun than we were. Lacy and I visited, and when we got tired of licking the yucky-tasting envelopes, we tried on some of Lacy's clothes and looked at the new J. Crew catalog. Emily and I were supposed to leave around five-thirty so we could have dinner ready for Daddy. But when Lacy and I went downstairs, her mom and my mom were no place in sight. We hunted all through the house, calling for them. Finally, Lacy spotted them out in the garden near the pool. They were cutting flowers to replace those in the vases around the Valentines' home.

"You know, Courtney," Emily said as she drove to our house, "Pamela has the most beautiful home. The flowers just make the place. I think we should work on the flower beds around our place. You know, get them ready for spring. Throw in some peat moss and plant a few bulbs. What do you think?"

"Sounds great, Mom." As I said it, I felt the corners of my mouth tug toward my ears. It was the first time I had called Emily "Mom"—not because I had to but because it . . . well, it just seemed natural.

Friday night, I slept over at Lacy's. We worked on party favors and made sure everything looked neat and tidy around the pool. We stacked the CDs that we were going to dance to by the stereo. Then we talked and laughed and giggled. It was two in the morning when Mrs. Valentine finally came in to Lacy's bedroom.

"I know you two have a lot to talk about," she said in a sleepy voice. "And I do plan to let you sleep late in the morning—but this is *ridiculous!* Go to sleep!"

Lacy and I nestled into her water bed. As soon as Mrs. Valentine left, Lacy leaned toward my ear.

"I've got to tell you something," she whispered, "but you have to promise not to tell."

"Okay," I whispered back.

"I mean, *really promise*," she insisted. "You can't tell anybody. Not even your mom. Swear?"

Even though I knew she couldn't see, I made an X across my chest with my finger.

"I swear. What is it?"

"My mom's pregnant."

My eyes flashed wide. "For real?" I gasped.

"For real. She's expecting in February. But, I mean it. You can't tell anybody. It's just our secret. Promise?"

"Promise."

We giggled and talked some more, but we spoke in whispers, our voices softer and softer, until we finally fell asleep.

The big Saturday-night back-to-school party turned out to be kind of a dud. For some reason, the actual party wasn't nearly as exciting or as much fun as all the planning that Lacy and I had done over the past two weeks. The boys wouldn't dance. After we swam in Lacy's pool and ate chips and cake, they kind of clumped together over on one side of the patio. They talked and stared at us girls, who were clumped together on the other side. Then they scuffled and wrestled with each other.

A couple of the girls danced. Brandy and Beth Simms looked weird, dancing together. But Lacy and I joined them anyway, hoping it would get some of the boys moving.

It didn't work.

There were a bunch of adults who were there, too. Mom and Daddy came to help the Valentines supervise the party. Mrs. Carter came, also. Just about everyone in our homeroom was there. Well, except for Greg and Joshua. Lacy and I agreed that it would be better not to have those two. Judy got an invitation, but she didn't show up. Neither did La Shea. When I asked Lacy about her, she said she must have forgotten to send the invitation.

Despite the boys, we had fun anyway. When the party was over Daddy, Mom, and I stayed around to help clean up. As we were leaving, Lacy pointed at her own tummy. Then she pointed at her mother. She winked and put a finger to her lips.

I nodded to let her know I understood.

All through the party, I had been dying to tell Brandy or just anyone. I didn't. What Lacy had told me was important—like a sacred trust—something that you would only tell to your closest friend. I kept my promise.

It made me feel warm and toasty inside to realize she trusted me so much. To have a friend like Lacy—well, it made me smile.

Four months later, when we went back to school after Christmas vacation, I was still smiling. This was the best—the very best—year I'd ever had!

For Christmas I'd been given a silk skirt and blouse, a denim blouse, a pair of Cole-Haan clogs and a bulky, wool rag-sweater that I *loved*. Mom picked them out and I really felt pretty in them. Ben got me a choker necklace with a little diamond in the center. He told me it wasn't a real diamond, but I thought it was beautiful anyway. Daddy gave me my own heavy-duty, chromed, socket set. It even had an extender for reaching the hard-to-get-to places behind a motor block. Lacy found some bath soap that smelled pretty strong. She said it was Musk and the guys would "totally dig it." Lacy was my best friend, so I put my Vel soap in a dish by the sink and used the musk stuff.

I couldn't ever remember being so happy. Daddy was happy, too. That made me even happier. Ben and Mom still didn't get along. But with Ben having gone to football practice in the fall and now basketball, and Emily working late in Dallas, they weren't around one another much, so they didn't fight. Mom and I worked in our garden on the days she did get home early. I loved flowers, and I loved having her with me as we worked to get our flowerbeds ready for spring.

The fighting at school had stopped, too. Joshua left Judy alone. And both he and Greg Bowlin settled down some. I think that was mostly because of Bobby Bozworth.

One day, right before Thanksgiving, Racita Minendez had started crying because somebody had swiped a card she'd gotten for her mother. Usually, when things came up missing from our room, you could count on either Greg or Joshua having had something to do with it. Bobby marched right over to Greg and told him to give Racita's card back. When Greg said he didn't have it, Bobby picked his desk up (with him still in it) and dumped the stuff in the desk and Greg right out on the floor. Sure enough, there was the card. The whole class burst out laughing, watching Greg flop around on the floor. We just barely got quiet before Mrs. Hooper got back to the room. Greg and Joshua didn't mess around much after that. Well, at least not with the people in our room.

Life was a lot easier and a lot more fun without people fighting all the time.

I think the thing that made me smile the most was cheerleading. Lacy, six other girls, and I made the sixth-grade cheerleading team. Not that we really had anybody to cheer for. Sixth graders didn't get to go out for any sports, and since there weren't any games or stuff, mostly cheerleading was just practice.

Then right after football season, two of the eighth-grade girls got kicked off the cheerleading squad. Nobody really knew why. Gossip on the playground had it that they either couldn't get along with Miss Tipton, who was the sponsor, or because their grades dropped. Whatever the reason, it didn't matter. Miss Tipton needed eight girls for the squad. She came and watched the sixth graders practice a few times and . . .

Lacy and I were picked to move up.

It was like being real, honest-to-goodness cheerleaders. We got to practice with the seventh- and eighth-grade girls. We got uniforms—white blouses and short, blue skirts with a gold band around the waist. We even had our own pom-poms. It was great.

When I told Daddy about it, he was proud of me. He jumped up and hugged me and kissed me and kind of raced around the house. First thing I knew, he got on the phone and called Dexter's dad, Mr. Langley, then all the guys from his shop, to brag about his daughter becoming a real Blyle Junior High School cheerleader.

Daddy was every bit as proud of me as he'd been of Ben when he was picked as the starting quarterback for the football team.

"You got the world by the tail, Courtney." He'd laughed and hugged me again. "Got the world by the tail."

We practiced every Monday, Tuesday, and Wednesday afternoon, from the time football season was over until Christmas. Lacy's mom picked us up after practice each day. That was great, too, because I didn't have to ride the bus. And after practice, we usually spent an hour or so over at her house, listening to CDs or talking about boys. Finally, we worked on our studies until her mom or dad drove me home. We even met three days during the holidays. Lacy's brother in California sent her some neat outfits for Christmas. We tried them on and flipped around in front of the mirror, laughing at ourselves and each other so much that our stomachs hurt.

The second Thursday in January, the seventh-

and eighth-grade boys were to play a basketball game. It was the first time Lacy and I would have to perform in front of a real crowd. I did fine all day. Then, right before school was out and we went back to homeroom for announcements, Mr. Riley, the principal, talked to us over the intercom.

He fussed about the noise in the halls and the lunchroom. He told us that someone had been stealing art supplies from the art room and that the person *would* be caught and "severely punished" unless he or she returned the things immediately. Then he reminded everyone to bring money for school pictures the following week. And finally, he said: "Don't forget we have a home basketball game tonight. I hope everyone will come and show some school spirit by supporting our boys and our cheerleaders."

Lacy glanced at me from her desk at the front of the room. She gave me a thumbs-up signal. I tried to smile back, but I couldn't. Theresa Dayton was at the desk next to Lacy's. She gave me the okay sign, but she didn't smile. At lunch recess, Theresa had clunked herself on the head when she'd tried to throw her baton up and catch it. Lacy and I had taken her to the office to get an ice pack. She still held the thing on top of her head.

"What a klutz," Lacy had said when we'd left

Theresa with the nurse. "Clumsy nerd is gonna kill herself with that thing."

The announcements were over. For a second the room was quiet. But to me, the word cheerleader echoed over and over in my head. I could still hear Lacy calling Theresa a clumsy nerd.

Cheerleader. Clumsy nerd. Cheerleader—that was me, too.

Suddenly, panic grabbed hold of me. It clung to me, wrapping around me like a thick fog. My head felt clammy. I couldn't breathe. I felt dizzy.

"Courtney?"

The sound of Judy's voice made me blink. I glanced at her. She frowned and tilted her head.

"Courtney, you okay?"

I took a deep breath. My eyes crossed, but I wasn't quite as dizzy anymore.

Judy flicked the tip of her cane and tapped me gently on the knee.

"Hey, Courtney, you all right?"

I blinked, then focused on her pretty brown eyes.

"I'm gonna make a complete fool of myself tonight," I gasped. "I can't remember any of the routines and . . . and . . ."

Judy gave a little laugh.

"You're gonna do fine. You're just a little nervous."

"LITTLE NERVOUS???" my voice squeaked. "I'm not nervous. I'm scared to death. I just know I'm gonna mess up. The older girls know it, too. None of them likes me. They hardly even talk to Lacy and me. Well . . . Nancy Osoki's nice . . . but the rest of them are always saying how dumb and clumsy I am and . . . and . . ."

Judy flicked her cane out and whacked my leg again. This time it was a little harder than before. I jumped. Her face and her eyes were stern.

"Calm down, you're gonna do fine. It doesn't matter what the rest of the girls think. You're good. You're gonna do just fine. Now, relax."

I took another deep breath.

"But . . . but what if I mess up . . . or . . . or . . ." The most *horrible* thought in the world flashed before my eyes. "What if I fall down?"

Judy looked at me. It was the weirdest look I'd ever seen. It made me feel like I'd just asked the dumbest question in the whole wide world.

"If you fall down, just get up and keep going."

Ben picked me up after school because his practice was shorter than usual. Dexter was in the front seat.

"Hey, General George," he greeted as I opened

the door and collapsed in the back. "You're gonna knock 'em dead tonight at the game. General George is gonna be the cutest cheerleader on the whole floor."

I gave a weak smile.

The guy named Ronald was in the backseat next to me. I smiled and nodded at him. He nodded back, but he didn't smile. He just sat there, clutching his sports bag and looking cross and grumpy.

After we let Ronald and Dexter off at their homes, I confided in Ben about how scared I was. At first he just sort of laughed at me like Judy had done. Then, when he figured out how *really* scared I was, he reached over and ruffled my hair.

"The first football game, I felt the same way," he said. "Juniors don't usually get to be starting quarterback. A lot of the seniors gave me a hard time at practice, and I figured they'd miss their blocks or stuff like that—just to let the other team knock me around. You know, prove to the coach that a junior really wasn't good enough to be there.

"I was more scared than you. Shoot, I threw up twice before the game even started. But once we got out there on the field—once the guys saw that I really could play—well . . . You're gonna be the same. Once you get started, you'll show 'em. You'll do fine."

"Promise?"

"I promise." He kind of laughed and ruffled my hair again. "You got nothing to worry about, kid. I've seen you practice. You're good. You're gonna do great. You got the world by the tail."

When he said that, it made me smile. It was the same old-fashioned, corny expression that Daddy used when I told him I was going to be a cheer-leader.

"Courtney, you got the world by the tail."

It was a dumb thing to say. The world didn't have a tail. Now dogs or snakes—they had tails—but not the world.

I remembered that once when I was little, I grabbed hold of the neighbor's dog by its tail. The darned thing turned around and bit me.

Maybe that's the trouble when you got something by the tail.

CHAPTER

10

I did fine. Once I got out on the floor and started, all the routines we'd learned in practice came back. It was perfect. Well, almost. On one cartwheel I landed sort of crooked. But I did like Judy said. I got up and kept going. Nobody seemed to notice.

Daddy and Ben were there in the crowd. Dexter and his folks came to watch me, too. I think Dexter and his mother cheered louder than anyone. Mrs. Langley even waved her handkerchief in big circles around her head when I got out to do a cheer.

The next day, almost everybody in Mrs. Hooper's homeroom came up and told Lacy and me how well we'd done. Even Mrs. Hooper said she was impressed. On the way to lunch, Peter Morrison stopped me in the hall. He used to sit next to me in fifth grade. I thought Peter Morrison was cute. He was even cuter now. Peter was also the only sixth grader who got to play on the seventh- and eighth-grade Blyle basketball team.

"You did good last night, Courtney." He kind of punched me on the arm and winked.

He winked!

Peter Morrison winked at me!!!

My face got all hot.

Daddy and Ben were right. I had the world by the tail.

Then . . . sure enough . . .

I guess it all started at lunch recess.

Lacy and I spent a little longer than usual in the lunchroom. We weren't really busy eating. We were just sitting around longer than normal, so people could come by our table and tell us how well we did at the game. When we got outside, a big crowd had gathered near the basketball court. Some seventh-grade girls and some of the girls who went to Bedford last year were sitting on *our* parallel bars.

Lacy was so cool.

She simply marched up and glared at the sixth-grade girls from Bedford. She didn't even have to say anything. She just sort of looked at them and they hopped down and went to stand someplace else. Nancy Osoki and two other seventh-grade girls were on the end of the bars closest to the basketball court. Lacy hopped up next to Nancy and scooted close.

"What's going on?"

Nancy looked around. When she saw me, she slid over and patted the bar next to her. I climbed up between her and Lacy.

"Last night at the game, Tim Barum kept getting fouled. Remember?"

Lacy and I nodded. (I really didn't remember. I had been so worried about what I was doing I hadn't even watched the game.)

"Tim missed every single free throw," Nancy went on. "In Mr. Polk's social studies class, a bunch of the guys got to razzing him about it. He got so mad, he almost started a fight, right there in the class. Anyway, Mr. Polk came down the hall before they began throwing punches, so Tim challenged some of the guys to a free-throw contest. He said he'd pay five dollars to anybody who could beat him. Figure if anybody beats him, he'll pay 'em the five dollars, then later, he'll try to beat 'em up."

Nancy nudged me with her elbow. "The way Tim shoots free throws, I think everybody's hanging around to watch the fight." She smiled and turned back toward the basketball court. I liked Nancy. Of all the girls in cheerleading, Nancy was the nicest. When the others called Lacy and me clumsy or dumb, Nancy just ignored them and showed us how to do stuff.

It didn't take long to get bored watching the boys shoot baskets. Tim would take ten shots. He usually made either five or six. Then one of the other seventh-grade boys would strut up to the free-throw line and only make three or four shots. It didn't look like there was going to be a fight.

Theresa Dayton hopped down from the bars and found an empty spot behind the crowd where she could practice her twirling.

She was really getting pretty good at spinning the silver-colored baton around. She could pass it from one hand to the other, between her legs, and even make it go round and round her neck by balancing it with her arms and elbows. But when it came to throwing the thing, she hadn't improved a bit.

Theresa tossed it as high as she could. It spun and glistened in the noonday sun. She scampered around, making sure she was under it as it started down. She watched. She reached for it.

Then at the last second, she covered her head with her hands, squealed, and ran.

Only this time Theresa didn't run quick enough.

The big rubber tip on one end came down and jabbed her right on the bottom. She squealed again, grabbed her seat, and started jumping around.

Nancy and the other seventh-grade girls burst out laughing. Theresa kept hopping and rubbing her bottom. One of the girls across from Nancy laughed so hard that she fell off the bars. If she hadn't grabbed the rail with her hand, she would have landed on her head instead of her knees.

Lacy and I usually didn't laugh at Theresa. We were used to watching her scream and run out from under that dumb baton. But watching and listening to Nancy and the others got us tickled. We started laughing, too.

Theresa snatched her baton off the ground and marched over to the bars. She looked at the seventh graders. Then, deciding it was best not to mess with them, she stepped in front of Lacy and me.

"It's not funny," she complained, still rubbing her seat. "It hurt."

Lacy and I tried to look serious. It didn't work. Even though I forced the corners of my mouth down, a snorting sound crept out of my nose. I started laughing again.

"It's not funny," Theresa repeated. "Catching that baton is a lot harder than it looks and . . ."

Suddenly, she stopped talking. She glanced toward the basketball court where the free-throw competition was still going on. A little smile tugged at the corner of her mouth.

"I bet you can't throw it that high and catch it." She kind of puffed her chest out. "In fact, I'll pay anybody five dollars who can."

Lacy just sneered at her and brushed her away with a wave of her hand. Theresa turned to glare at me. "I'll pay five bucks," she repeated.

But before I could answer, Nancy jumped off the bars.

"I'll try it."

Two other seventh graders followed her. "Yeah, for five bucks—why not?"

I ended up fifth in line. Nancy and the two seventh graders were first, then Brandy squeezed in behind them before I could find a place.

Nancy caught the baton, but she didn't throw it very high. Her friends couldn't even get hold of it. Brandy almost caught the thing, but she didn't throw it high. She did get it, but it flipped around her hand and fell.

I picked the baton up and took a deep breath.

Before I could even think about throwing it, a loud roar of laughter came from the direction of the basketball court. We turned to see what had happened.

Balancing on her cane and dragging her legs behind, Judy Baird waddled up to the free-throw line. The laughter was so loud, it seemed to roll across the grounds like a spring thunderstorm. It didn't seem to bother Judy. She put her toes on the line. She teetered for a second, getting her balance, then slipped the cane behind her bottom. She leaned back on the top—using the thing like a prop or brace.

"You said you'd take on all comers." Judy smiled. "I want to try."

The seventh-grade basketball player named Tim Barum looked at her and shook his head. Then he shrugged and handed her the ball.

"Sure thing, kid, go for it."

Judy wiggled her bottom, making sure the cane was braced securely. She shot.

The laughter exploded again, only this time it was from surprise, since the basketball actually went in.

By the time Judy sank five baskets in a row, there was no more laughter. Now, all the kids who had gathered around were clapping and cheering. Tim's mouth gaped so wide that if he'd tried to walk, he would have tripped over his jaw. Of course, the other boys who had been shooting baskets had their mouths open, too.

Judy missed on her sixth basket. Everybody

moaned. Then she made seven and eight. Now, even Tim was clapping and cheering for her. I think everybody on the whole playground had stopped what they were doing to come gather around. Judy Baird made eight of ten free throws!

We couldn't believe it. Everybody clapped and cheered and screamed. Even the seventh-grade boys rushed up to pat Judy on the back and congratulate her. The crowd fell to a nervous silence when Tim Barum made his way over to her. For a second, he looked stern and mean. Then a soft smile wiggled across his face. Tim pulled a five-dollar bill from his pocket and presented it to Judy.

"They let baseball players have pinch hitters," he said as the clapping and cheers started again. "I wish basketball could have pinch free-throw shooters. With you on the team, we'd make the state play-offs for sure."

A bunch of people wanted Judy to shoot some more baskets. She adjusted her cane. Out of the second ten shots, she only made seven. On her third try, she made nine out of ten. The bell rang just as she sank her last basket. People cheered again and rushed to congratulate her, then started for the building.

Theresa Dayton stepped in front of me and cocked her eyebrows.

"Well?"

"Well, what?"

With the excitement of watching Judy, I'd forgotten the silver baton in my hand. I gave a sheepish grin, remembering.

"Oh, yeah."

There was a big rubber tip on one end and a small rubber tip on the other. I got hold of the end with the small tip, like Theresa always did, and threw it as hard as I could.

It spun round and round, a silver blur like the propeller of an airplane. And like an airplane, it climbed higher and higher into the blue sky. For an instant, it hesitated at the top of its arch—higher than anyone had ever thrown it before—then it started down.

It was partly Judy's fault. When I threw it, I remembered the laughter as Judy dragged herself to the free-throw line on the basketball court. I thought of her courage. The baton spun. I was amazed at her confidence. The baton fell faster and faster toward the ground. I moved so I would be right under it. Her courage was my inspiration. I reached up to catch the spinning, silver rod. If Judy, the little crippled girl, could shoot baskets, then surely I could catch this little . . .

CHAPTER

11

"What happened, Courtney?" Ben's voice was stern and worried.

I didn't answer.

Dexter turned around in the front seat and got on his knees. He reached back and took hold of my wrist. I pulled against his grip, but it was no use. He lifted my hand *and* the ice pack from my right eye.

"Man!" he gasped. "General George, you're gonna have one heck of a shiner!"

He let go, and I slapped the ice pack back on my face. My right eye still hurt. It throbbed so much I couldn't even open it. Ben had just pulled out from his parking spot. He jammed on the brakes.

"Who did it?" he growled.

"Yeah." Dexter spun around and opened his door. "Who was it? We'll go beat the . . ."

"I did it," I snarled back at them.

Dexter shut the door and both boys turned to stare at me.

"I did it," I repeated. "I was trying to throw Theresa Dayton's baton and I . . . well . . . I sort of misjudged when I tried to catch it and . . . ah . . ."

Ben put the car in gear and started off again. Dexter gave a little giggle, then slapped his hand over his mouth real quick. Even Ronald, who always looked like he'd been sucking on lemons, smiled. It was the first time I'd ever seen him grin.

"It's not funny," I snapped. "It hurts, and I look horrible."

That just made it worse.

I folded my arms and sulled up. It really wasn't funny. Nancy and her friends had to take me to the nurse, Mrs. Everly. Although Mrs. Everly said I'd be fine, I was convinced that the last thing I would ever see with that eye was the big white bulb on the end of Theresa Dayton's baton—right before it landed square in my eye and sent the stars spinning through my head.

Mrs. Everly kept me in the office until just before school was out. When I got back to Mrs. Hooper's homeroom, everybody seemed concerned. Then, when they found out I was going to be all right . . . well . . . giving yourself a black eye is kind of funny.

It's funny if it happens to somebody else.

Lacy Valentine didn't think it was funny at all. After the bell rang, she waited outside the door. I tried to smile as I walked past her. Lacy sighed.

"Cool move, Courtney. That black eye's going to look horrible when we're out in front of all those people Thursday night." She flipped around and prissed off down the hall. "Cheerleader with a black eye. That's just great."

Later that day, Daddy came home early from the shop so we could get ready for Ben's basketball game. He even smiled when I told him what had happened. Then he fixed a fresh ice bag for me. After we ate, Ben went to pick up Dexter and Ronald. Dad and I watched TV for a while, then we got ready. As Daddy checked to make sure the lights were off and the back door was locked, I remembered the announcement about school pictures next week. I was glad I did, because if I'd waited until Monday, I probably would have forgotten. Daddy gave me a ten and a five for the pictures, and I stuffed the money inside my homework paper and put that inside my geography book.

"Mom going to be home in time to see some of the game?" I asked.

Daddy shrugged. "Haven't heard from her. Probably had to work late with Jim again." He latched the front door. "How's the eye?"

"Fine," I lied, pretending to rub my forehead so I could cup my hand over it and hide the black-and-blue spot.

Well, it really didn't hurt quite as bad now as before, and I could open it just a little. Still, I watched most of Ben's game with my hand near my forehead, trying to hide my black eye from the people who sat around us.

Guys think they look cool when they have a black eye. To me it was totally embarrassing.

Emily was waiting for us when we got home. Like Lacy, she seemed more concerned about how I was going to look than about whether I was hurt or not. Daddy fixed us all a bowl of ice cream. Then, figuring Ben, Dexter, and Ronald would be out cruising late, we went to bed.

The sound of the telephone woke me. I yawned and blinked. It rang again. My left eye was the only one I could open. I propped myself up on my elbows and looked at the clock beside my bed. It said 12:40.

A sudden chill ran through me. No one ever

called us that late. I blinked again, this time so hard that my sore eye even opened. I sat straight up in bed.

"Hello," I heard Daddy say from the hall. "Yes, this is the Brown residence."

I kicked the sheets back and swung my feet over the edge of my bed.

"Yes, I am," Daddy said.

I staggered toward the door.

"Yes." Daddy's voice was much softer now.

I opened the door just as he hung up the phone. His face was pale. It scared me. The breath caught in my throat.

"Who was it, Daddy? What's wrong?"

He looked at me with sad eyes.

"It was the police," he said, wiping his nose with the back of his hand. "Ben's in jail."

CHAPTER

12

It really hurt when the baton landed on my right eye. Once, when we'd been playing soccer, Ryan Foster kicked the ball and it hit me in the stomach so hard that I doubled over and fell on the ground. It hurt so bad I couldn't even catch my breath. And last summer when I was helping pull the oil plug under the Corvette, the wrench slipped and I ripped half the skin off my knuckles. I cried and cried.

The hurt that caught hold of me when Daddy said, "Ben's in jail" was lots, lots worse than any of those things.

My insides hurt. My heart seemed to throb, deep down in my chest. I could hear it pounding in my ears. Nobody in our family had ever been in jail. Never! It was a horrible place where horrible people were sent—scuzzy, dirty people, like the guys who hung around the bars down in Ryland Heights. Bad people were put in jail. People who did mean and nasty things to hurt other people. Ben wasn't like that. Ben couldn't be in jail. Not my brother, he just couldn't. I forced my tears back.

Mom peeked from the bedroom as Daddy hung up the phone.

"I tried to warn you." She folded her arms. "The way that boy back-talks me and runs around with those blacks—I tried to warn you."

I felt my fist clench at my side. It made me mad when Emily said that. And, all of a sudden, I realized I was thinking of her as "Emily" again and not as "Mom."

Daddy went to get dressed, and I followed him down the hall. At the door of his and Emily's room, I caught the sleeve of his pajamas and tugged.

"It's got to be some kind of mistake, Daddy. Ben's good. So's Dexter. It's just a big mistake."

Daddy leaned down and kissed me on the forehead.

"It's a mistake," he agreed confidently. "We'll get it all straightened out. Don't worry."

Daddy left for the police station after telling Emily and me to get some sleep. "There's nothing you can do," he said. Emily went back to bed, still muttering, "I told you so." It made me so mad I wanted to spit right in her eye. I couldn't. I couldn't sleep either. I tried, but I finally gave up and went to watch out the front door.

It was nearly daylight when Daddy got home.

Ben wasn't with him.

I fixed Daddy a pot of coffee, like I used to do after Mama died and before he married Emily. I had to make him sit down and tell me what happened. He kept looking at his watch. Then he sighed and took a sip of his coffee.

"After the game, Ben drove Dexter and that kid, Ronald, down to the Sonic for fries and a Coke," he began. "The Ronald kid hopped out to say 'Hi' to some friends. He came back and after a little while, he got out again to go speak to some other people.

"Ben and Dexter said they didn't think anything about it. Then when they finished eating and started to drive off . . . well, Ben said three police cars came flying up with their lights flashing. The patrolmen jumped out—guns drawn and everything. I think they scared Ben and Dexter to death." He stopped, looking at his watch, then the clock on the stove.

"Why?" I asked. "Why did the cops do that to Ben?"

Daddy sighed.

"Evidently the Ronald guy they were with had been selling drugs. And evidently, one of the guys he sold them to the second time he got out was an undercover narcotics detective. They dug around in the sports bag he had and found six vials of crack cocaine. The cops arrested all three of the boys on drug charges."

A picture of Ronald and that sports bag flashed through my mind's eye. I remember how he was always clutching it when I got in the car, instead of throwing it in the pile with Ben's and Dexter's bags. I remembered how he hung on to the thing, looking sour and surly.

A plopping sound chased the picture from my head. Daddy and I both looked up. Emily staggered into the kitchen. Her bare feet made the plopping sound on the linoleum as she waddled to the coffee pot.

"Well, what did old Ben do this time?" she slurred as she poured herself a cup of coffee. "He get in a fight or get drunk or something?"

I cringed when she said that. Daddy glanced at his watch again and started his story over for her.

". . . and they found six vials of crack cocaine in Ronald's sports bag. Dexter's parents, Paul and Beverly, were there with me," he went on. "Since Paul's a mechanic in the police garage, most of the patrolmen know him and Beverly. The cops seem like pretty nice guys. But they explained to us that because the arrest was drug related, they couldn't release the boys to their parents like they usually do with juveniles. They said the boys would probably have to stay in custody until Monday when a judge will set their bail and do a preliminary hearing."

"What's that?" I asked.

"It's where a judge decides if there's enough evidence to take the case to trial," Daddy said. "Anyway, since the police know Paul and Beverly, one of the detectives called a judge. He agreed to come in before Monday. He'll be in at ten this morning to set their bail so we can get Ben out of there." He looked at his watch, then at Emily. "Got any cash?"

Suddenly, Emily was wide-awake. She'd listened to the story about Ben with half-open eyes. Now her eyes were round and as wide as her coffee cup.

"I . . . ah . . . well," she stuttered. "There's probably a twenty and some ones in my purse. Why?"

Daddy put his elbows on the table and rested his chin in his hands.

"The patrolmen said the bail would probably be between fifteen hundred and five thousand dollars. The courts won't take checks. You have to have cash or a money order or something like that. Soon as the bank opens at nine, I need to get some cash so we can get him home. I'm not sure there's enough money in our account. That's why I hoped you had some cash."

Emily snapped to her feet.

"You . . . you . . . you're going to the bank? You . . . well you ought to just leave him there. It'll teach him a lesson."

Daddy glared at her.

"I can't believe you said that, Emily," he gasped. "Ben and Dexter didn't know anything about the drugs. They didn't even know that Ronald had the stuff. The only reason that kid was with them was because they were trying to keep him interested in sports so he *wouldn't* get into a gang or start messing with drugs. I can't believe . . ."

Emily slammed her coffee cup on the table so hard that some of the brown liquid sloshed out.

"I don't have to take that tone of voice from you or anyone." She spun and stormed toward the bedroom. "I just won't tolerate the yelling—the abuse."

My mouth fell open. I watched her stalk away and turned to Daddy. He was gaping in disbelief, too.

"Was I yelling at her?"

"No. Well, you were talking a little loud, but you weren't yelling."

Daddy shook his head, like he was rattling around some loose marbles in there or something. Then he looked at his watch. "Quarter of nine. I got to go."

"Me, too." I jumped up from the table.

Daddy looked at me and shook his head.

"No. I don't want you around that jail or down at the courthouse. You just stay here with . . ."

I planted my fists firmly on my hips, squinting at him. "I'm going. Ben needs me. I'll wait in the car, but I got to be there when he comes out. I got to let him know that I love him and don't believe he did anything wrong. I'm going!" A sudden shiver grabbed at my elbows. It raced up my arms and across my shoulder blades. "And even if he did do wrong, he's my brother . . . and . . . and he needs to know I love him anyway."

CHAPTER

13

I didn't have to argue with Daddy for very long. I guess he was in a rush to get to the bank and figured it was easier to let me go than trying to talk me into staying home with Emily. I waited in the car, like I promised.

We got to the bank just as the uniformed guard was unlocking the door. Daddy parked the car and leaped out. He bounded up the steps.

Twenty minutes later, when Daddy came out, he wasn't bounding. He walked on slow, shuffling feet. His head was bowed low and his shoulders drooped. No matter how much I pestered or how many times I asked, he didn't tell me what was wrong until we parked at the courthouse and he started to get out.

"The checking account has been closed. It's gone," he sort of breathed, instead of talking to me. "Not a single penny left in it. We're broke. I don't have time to go home and ask Emily about it. The judge is coming in at ten."

I didn't stop shaking from the time he got out of the car until he came back, almost two hours later.

He came back without Ben.

I'd never seen my daddy look so sad and worried.

"The bail was fifteen hundred dollars." He sighed. "Paul Langley said he'd loan me the money, but by the time the hearing . . . well . . . it's almost noon. The banks close at noon on Saturday."

"Ben can't come home?"

Daddy shook his head and looked even sadder and more worried than before. But by the time we got home, he didn't look sad and worried anymore. Daddy was mad.

His eyes were scrunched almost shut. His jaw stuck out like a bulldog's. Daddy slammed the car door and marched to the house. I followed, hot on his heels.

"Emily!" he roared as he opened the front door. "What happened to the checking account? You couldn't have spent all that money. Emily?

"Emily?

"Emily, where are you?"

Daddy went through every room of our house, calling her name. Emily didn't answer.

*   *   *

I was the one who found the note. It was in an envelope on the mantel. I gave it to Daddy. As he started reading it, he sort of collapsed into his recliner. The more he read, the deeper he sank into the chair. I bit my lip. I felt the trembling run through me as I watched him.

It was like watching someone die. The life just seemed to flow out of him. After he finished, his arm and the note dangled limply beside his chair. The little piece of paper slipped from his fingers and fluttered to the floor.

When I picked it up, Daddy didn't even seem to notice. He just stared straight ahead. His eyes— happy eyes that always sparkled—looked empty.

I read the note in my hand.

Dear David,

I know the timing is terrible, but I'm leaving you. Jim Parker and I are in love.

Neither of us meant for it to happen, but working together and being together like we were . . . well, it just did. I am sorry. Jim has sold his share of the real-estate agency and we are leaving to start anew in a different state. You have been a good husband, but I must follow my heart. I know this is a shock, but in time you will get over me and find another.

> *Sincerely,*
> *Emily*

P.S. Sorry about the checking account. When we get on our feet, I'll try to repay you.

I stared at the note. The word "Sincerely" seemed to burn itself into my mind. Not "Love," not "Please forgive me," not even "Best wishes." Emily had just signed it "Sincerely." It looked like a business letter we had to write one time in school. How could anyone be so cold?

I flopped down on the couch. I looked at the note. I looked at my daddy. There was nothing I could do to help.

My brother was in jail and we didn't have the money to get him out. Emily had left us—and just like Ben had warned me back at the beginning of school—she'd broken my daddy's heart. And there was nothing I could say. Nothing I could do to help. All I could do was hurt.

I hurt for Ben. My insides hurt for Daddy. I'd never felt so helpless and sad. Nothing that ever happened, nothing that could ever happen, would make me feel worse than I did at that very moment.

CHAPTER

14

Monday morning, things got worse.

The weekend was the longest one I had ever spent. I tried to talk to Daddy. I watched TV, but I really didn't see or listen to what was on. I just kept thinking about Ben being stuck in jail. I didn't sleep Saturday night. I tossed and turned and looked at the clock every twenty minutes or so. Sunday night, I guess I was so exhausted I got a little rest.

Daddy spent the whole weekend slumped in his chair. I tried to get him to bed Saturday night, but he wouldn't go. When I got up Sunday morning, he was still there. I wanted to talk to him. I offered to get him something to eat. He didn't answer. I brewed a pot of coffee for him. He only sat there with a sad look on his face and with his empty eyes staring straight ahead.

The only time he so much as moved was when I was getting ready to catch the bus for school. On the way out the door, I opened my geography book and found the fifteen dollars he had given me for class pictures. I held it out to him, thinking maybe it would help get Ben out of jail. He blinked. His eyes focused on the money in my hand.

"No," he said.

"I don't want my picture taken," I protested. "I've got a black eye and I look horrible. Besides, Ben . . ."

Daddy folded my hand around the bills.

"I want you to get your picture."

He looked at the clock, then his eyes went blank and empty again.

I guess I was still in a daze when I walked into Mrs. Hooper's room. I didn't notice how everybody was staring at me and talking in hushed whispers. Not at first anyway. When I finally did, I knew how Judy must have felt back at the beginning of school, with everybody staring at her and talking behind her back.

It shouldn't have surprised me that people knew.

Lots of high-school kids hung out at the Sonic after Friday-night games. And a bunch of the high-school kids had younger brothers and sisters who went to Blyle. By lunchtime, probably everybody in school would know that Ben was in jail.

I reached up and cupped my hand to hide my black eye.

"How's the eye?"

Without moving my hand, I glanced up. Judy stood, teetering on her cane beside me.

I shrugged.

She leaned against my desk to help keep her balance. She looked worried.

"How's your brother? Did he get to come home yet?"

I shook my head, then frowned.

"How'd you hear about it?"

"It's all over school, Courtney." She sighed. "Don't worry about it. It doesn't matter what people say or gossip about. It just matters if you and your family are okay. Is there anything I can do?"

I wiped away a tear and told Judy everything. I even told her about the note and about Emily leaving my daddy.

Every now and then, Brandy Craig would scoot her chair over. But if I glanced at her, she'd turn around real quick like she wasn't really trying to listen. She never said anything to me. At the front of the room, Theresa Dayton kept leaning over and whispering to Lacy. They'd both look around and Theresa would giggle. Then Lacy would whisper something to her.

It made me mad. As soon as Judy went to sit at her desk, I started to get up. It didn't matter if Lacy was the most popular girl in sixth grade, she was still supposed to be my best friend. Best friends don't sit around and talk about you, they come back and ask if you're okay. I figured Lacy needed to know that.

I didn't even get my bottom out of the chair before Greg Bowlin came flying through the door. He was running so fast that he slipped when he tried to turn and dash down the aisle. He bounced off the teacher's desk, scrambled to his feet, and charged for his desk. He'd just landed in his chair when Larry Don jumped into his chair. He didn't even have time to warn us that Mrs. Hooper was about to appear at the door.

"Greg!" She pointed a finger as she came in. "You get to the office right this minute."

Greg tried to look innocent.

"Why? I didn't do nothin'. I've been sittin' right here . . ."

He wasn't too convincing, seeing as how he was

still panting and out of breath from running down the hall.

"I saw you, Greg." Mrs. Hooper glared at him. "You stuck your finger in the water fountain and sprayed water all over the hall and half the kids who were standing around. You get down to the office . . ."

"But . . ."

She folded her arms. Her right foot patted the floor.

"RIGHT NOW!!!"

Head bowed, Greg shuffled across the room. At the door, he paused to look at Mrs. Hooper. She jabbed her finger toward the office again, and he went on his way like someone who'd been playing in the rain and had a half-ton of mud on his shoes.

Mrs. Hooper was still in a huff when she sat down behind her desk and unfolded a computer sheet she'd brought with her from the office.

"Supposed to do lunchroom duty, play policewoman in the halls, and now . . ." she muttered, ". . . now, take up picture money. When am I supposed to teach school?"

She looked up, suddenly realizing how quiet everyone was. Clearing her throat, she glared back at the computer sheet.

"Everyone who has picture money, please line up by my desk."

"I ain't got no picture money," Joshua called from the back of the room.

Mrs. Hooper shot him a disgusted look.

"You *don't* have *any* picture money," she corrected. "Don't worry about it, Joshua." Then to the rest of us: "If you don't have picture money today, you can bring it Tuesday or Wednesday. Now, let's get this done so we can start class."

I got the fifteen dollars out of my geography book and followed Judy to the end of the line. When it was my turn, I handed Mrs. Hooper my money and started back to my desk.

"Courtney."

I heard her say my name, but I guess I was so busy twirling a strand of hair around my finger and trying to hide behind my hand that I didn't answer her.

"Courtney." She called my name again.

I turned. With the end of her pencil, Mrs. Hooper pointed at the helper chart next to the bulletin board by the door.

"Courtney Brown" was the name on the card.

"You're helper this week, Courtney." She handed me the envelope. "Run this to the office for me."

I took the brown envelope and headed down the hall. Just as I reached the office door, I hesitated. I opened the envelope.

There was a whole bunch of money inside. A glob

of fives and tens and twenties were smushed up in the bottom of the little envelope. I reached in and took out a five and a ten.

I didn't want my picture taken—not with a black eye. We needed the money. Emily was gone and Ben was in jail. I remembered Ben saying something about how Daddy owed the bank a lot of money or he might lose the shop. I looked at the money in my hand. Fifteen dollars wasn't much, but I could tell Mrs. Hooper to take my name off the picture list and give it to Daddy and . . .

. . . and then, I remembered the look on Daddy's face when I tried to give him the money earlier. I remembered how he wrapped my hands around it and told me he wanted me to have my picture.

So I stuffed the money back in the envelope and opened the office door.

Mrs. Ingle, our school secretary, wasn't at her desk. I expected to find Greg Bowlin in the chair by Mr. Riley's office. Greg wasn't there. In fact, the whole office was empty. I didn't stop to give it much thought. I put the picture envelope on the desk and hurried back to class.

CHAPTER

15

Classes weren't too bad. Our teachers kept us busy so people didn't have time to keep staring at me or whispering behind my back. Going between classes wasn't too cool. In the halls, I could feel everyone's eyes on me and hear the hushed whispers. It was terrible.

Lunch was the worst.

When the bell finally rang, I scurried down the hall. I simply had to tell Lacy what had happened. I had to talk to her and make her understand that Ben didn't have anything to do with drugs or anything bad like that. Lacy would understand. She was my friend.

But when I picked up my tray from the serving line and got to our table, Brandy Craig was already sitting in my chair beside Lacy. All the chairs at our table were full. I stood for a moment, feeling confused and lost. Finally, Lacy glanced around. She didn't say anything, just sort of tilted her head and looked down her nose.

I didn't say anything either. Head hung low, I went to the table where Brandy used to sit and took her spot. None of the girls there so much as said "Hi." They kept visiting with each other, totally ignoring me. They treated me like I wasn't even there. I didn't eat.

It was no big surprise when I got outside and found the bars full where I always sat. There was no spot for me. I marched up to Lacy. For the first time all day, I took my hand from my black eye and folded my arms.

"I've got to talk to you, Lacy. I have to tell you what happened and . . ."

She looked right over the top of my head.

"Not right now, I'm watching the game."

I glanced behind me. There wasn't even a game going on. There was just a bunch of boys standing around visiting.

"But, Lacy, please, I need to tell you what happened with Ben and . . ."

She shooed me away with a wave of her hand.

"Later, Courtney. I'm busy."

"But . . ."

She looked down the tip of her nose at me. "Later!"

When I walked away from the bars and all my "friends," my toes dragged along the ground, leaving little trails behind me. I wandered around and finally ended up in the middle of the playground. Standing like some little lost puppy, I felt tears begin to well up in my eyes.

The first drop of water hadn't squeezed out and down my cheek when there was a sudden sting on my bottom. I jumped and grabbed my seat. I spun around.

Judy stood there, balanced on her cane.

"Nobody's playing on the sixth-grade courts," she said. "Let's go shoot some baskets."

I shook my head.

She lifted her cane and threatened to swat me on the bottom again.

"Better come on." Her brown eyes sparkled.

I covered my seat and stepped away from her. "I can't shoot baskets. I'm no good at it."

Judy gave a little laugh and pointed at me with her stick.

"Not much good at tossing a baton either. All you need is some practice. Now, come on."

Reluctantly, I followed her across the grounds. I was right, I wasn't much good at shooting baskets.

But it kept my mind off my problems for a while. La Shea joined us and we talked and chased the ball. For just a few moments, I felt a little better. In fact, I felt better clear up until school was out and I went to cheerleading practice.

Once I got there, I turned into a total klutz.

I kept forgetting my routines and kept bumping into the other girls. We'd been practicing a pyramid, but when Pauline Reichter started to climb to the top, I sort of lost my balance. The whole pyramid crumbled. Pauline got up off the ground, rubbing her elbow.

"Dumb sixth grader," she grumped.

Even Miss Tipton said something about how I needed to concentrate and quit messing around.

After practice was finished, Nancy Osoki came over and put her arm around me. "I know you got a lot of problems right now," she said. "Got a lot going on and lots to worry about. Things are gonna be okay, Courtney. It'll be better tomorrow."

Lacy was already outside when I got there. She was talking to her mom. I opened the door and hopped in the backseat. The instant I sat down both of them stopped talking. I planned to tell her about Ben as soon as we got to her house. I'd make her listen to me instead of listening to CDs or looking through magazines.

We didn't go to Lacy's house. Mrs. Valentine drove me straight home. I sat in the backseat, and neither one of them said so much as one single word to me. They never even looked back. I got out, and the minute I shut the door, they drove off quickly down the street. My shoulders sagged. I pulled my book bag along the ground as I started toward the house.

Then, the best thing that could possibly have happened—happened.

"Hey, squirt, how come you look like your tail's draggin'?"

It was Ben's voice. I blinked. My heart pounded in my chest. He held the front door open and smiled at me.

I dropped my book bag at the edge of the street and raced toward him. Ben stepped out on the porch. When he saw how fast I was coming, he hopped down from the top step and stood, braced on the sidewalk.

I leaped into his outstretched arms and hugged his neck. He squeezed me back. I hugged and kissed my big brother as hard and as fast as I could. I laughed and cried, both at the same time. Ben laughed, too. I couldn't tell if he cried or not, because I clung to his neck so tight I couldn't see his face.

"That's enough, squirt," he said after a long, long time, "you're gettin' my face all wet."

He pried me loose and we sat on the front steps.

Ben told me that when they'd held the hearing this morning, the policemen who'd stopped the car told the judge that Ronald tried to run when all the lights and sirens started, but Ben and Dexter just sat there, looking dumb and confused. They all agreed that my brother and his friend didn't have any idea what was going on. Then Ben told about the detective who bought the drugs from Ronald and how after talking to all three of the boys, he felt that Ben and Dexter had no idea that Ronald even had drugs in the car. Coach Bentley, Ben's football coach, got up next. He told the judge about his concerns when Dexter and Ben started palling around with Ronald and how he had talked to both of them and even had their fathers come in to talk about it. He felt that all they were doing was trying to keep Ronald interested in sports so he wouldn't start running with the gangs. He told the judge that my brother and his friend were "real good boys" who would never get involved in drugs. They were just trying to help out a friend.

"The thing that really clinched it," Ben said, "was when Ronald's lawyer called for a recess." He looked at me kind of funny. "That's when they sort of call time out so they can go talk."

"Right." I scrunched up my nose and wobbled my head back and forth. "Like I thought recess meant they went out on the playground."

Ben gave a sheepish grin.

"Well, I just wanted to make sure you understood."

"I know what it means."

He smiled again. "Anyway, when the judge came back, he told us that Ronald and his lawyer pleaded guilty and said that Dexter and I knew nothing about him selling drugs.

"The judge sentenced Ronald to one year at the juvenile facility in Bay Town and three years' suspension. He told him that if he got arrested for possession or selling drugs within that three-year time, he'd try him as an adult and ship him off to the real prison at Huntsville. Then he dismissed all the charges against Dexter and me."

"And you get to be home." I smiled. Then a little ripple tweaked at my stomach. "When do you have to go back?"

A smile swept across my brother's face, stretching his skin so tight that it must have hurt. He shook his head. "No, squirt, we don't *ever* have to go back. 'Dismiss the charges' means the judge knows we were innocent. We're free. It's all over."

I wrapped my arms around his neck again and kissed him.

I could hardly wait to get back to school tomorrow. I could hardly wait to tell all my friends.

My feet never even touched the ground as I drifted down the hall Tuesday morning. It was like I was walking on a cloud. I'd never felt so light and free and happy.

I practically floated around the corner and into my classroom and . . .

Smack into Mrs. Hooper.

"Courtney," she said, sternly, "go to the office."

There was something about the look on her face that tugged my light smile clear down into my shoes. I cocked my head to the side.

"Huh?"

"Go to the office," she repeated, "RIGHT NOW!"

CHAPTER

16

The chair beside the doorway to Principal Riley's office had to be the loneliest spot on the face of the earth. That's where all the guys who got in trouble in class or on the grounds had to wait until the principal could get to them.

The teachers came and went. They said "Hi" to Mrs. Ingle, the school secretary, they visited with each other, then checked their mailboxes, or picked up stacks of work sheets for their class. They looked at me, sitting all alone in the chair, but they never spoke. If you were in the chair beside Mr. Riley's door, you were in trouble for something, and nobody was nice to you.

I kept telling myself that Mr. Riley just wanted to talk to me. Maybe he'd heard about Ben and might even make an announcement about how my brother was innocent. Then he'd tell everybody to quit talking about Ben behind my back. Maybe that's why Mrs. Hooper had sent me to the office.

But as I sat there, I realized that there was a big difference between being sent to the office and be-ing *sent* to the office.

There was something about the look on Mrs. Hooper's face when she pointed down the hall. There was even something about the way Mrs. In-gle was peeking over the top of her little gold-rimmed glasses at me. I felt like she was watching me. When she got up to put something in one of the teacher's mailboxes, she never seemed to take her eyes off me.

I felt like I sat in that chair for hours, but the big clock on the wall behind Mrs. Ingle showed I'd been there only four minutes before Mr. Riley opened his office door. A seventh-grade boy came shuffling out with his head hung low.

"I mean it, Carl," Mr. Riley's voice rumbled. "Any more problems on the bus, I'll suspend you for three days."

The boy scurried on his way and the principal looked at me.

"Courtney Brown?"

I nodded and tried to smile. The corners of my mouth didn't work.

"Yes, sir."

Mr. Riley opened the door a little wider. My

knees were shaking so hard they almost knocked together when I got up and walked through the open doorway. He closed the door and motioned me to a chair in front of the desk. As I sat, he walked to his chair on the opposite side. He looked at me for a moment—kind of like he was studying me or something. Then he held his hand out. Palm up, he reached across his desk toward me.

I frowned, not knowing what he wanted.

He leaned closer and wiggled his hand.

I tilted my head to the side. I didn't know whether he wanted me to shake hands with him or what. So I just sat, staring. Mr. Riley's face was mean.

"The money," he said finally when I didn't do anything, "we want it back."

My frown was so deep my bangs touched my eyebrows.

"What money?"

"The picture money." He wiggled his fingers and pushed his open palm at me. "We want it back, *now!*"

I'm glad I wasn't leaning forward. If I had been, my chin would have bumped his desk when my mouth flopped open. His palm crunched to a fist. Then he leaned back in his chair and folded his arms. He waited, and waited . . .

. . . and waited.

Finally, I held my hands out and shrugged help-lessly.

"I don't have any picture money today," I said. "Mrs. Hooper hasn't taken it up yet."

His jaw stuck out. "The picture money from yes-terday."

I shrugged again. "I gave it to Mrs. Ingle."

Mr. Riley leaned forward and put both hands on his desk. His elbows sort of bowed out and he re-minded me of the way a bulldog stands. "No, you didn't."

I sort of jerked, remembering.

"No," I agreed, "that's right. She wasn't in the office. I left it on her desk."

"You put the envelope and *some* of the money on the desk." He looked at me out of one eye. "What did you do with the rest of the money?"

"It . . . it was in the . . . envelope," I stammered. "It was all there."

Using his arms like the guys in gym doing push-ups, he shoved himself up from his chair.

"All right, you want to play it like that—fine."

He marched around his desk and flung the door open. "Mrs. Ingle, please call Coach Kompton on the intercom. Oh, I need Mrs. Hooper down here, too."

It must have been like a refrigerator in the principal's office. No matter how hard I tried, I couldn't stop shivering. The longer I waited for him to come back, the harder I shook. After an eternity, Mrs. Hooper, Coach Kompton, and Mrs. Ingle walked briskly into the room. Mr. Riley closed the door and strolled calmly to his desk. Mrs. Hooper sat in the chair beside me, Coach Kompton pulled up a chair from near the wall and faced me, next to Mr. Riley. Mrs. Ingle stood beside the principal.

"Mrs. Hooper," he began, "you took up the students' picture money yesterday morning, is that correct?"

"Yes, sir."

"And how many students paid?"

"Sixteen."

"And at fifteen dollars per student, what did the total come to?"

"Two hundred and forty dollars."

He glanced at the school secretary.

"Mrs. Ingle, when you totaled the picture money after school yesterday, what did you find?"

"Mrs. Hooper's envelope was eighty dollars short." She answered Mr. Riley, but she was looking at me. "I checked her figures three times."

"Are you sure there was two hundred and forty dollars in the envelope, Mrs. Hooper?"

"Yes, sir."

"And who brought the envelope to the office?"

Mrs. Hooper had her hands in her lap. She picked at her thumbnail and didn't look up.

"Courtney is the helper this week. She took the envelope down."

"Mr. Kompton?" We all looked at the boys' basketball coach. "Would you tell Miss Brown what you saw yesterday morning?"

Coach Kompton looked at me and shrugged.

"Well, I was headed down here to tell you about having to reschedule the game Thursday night. I was about halfway down the hall, and I saw this girl stop at the office door and open an envelope she had in her hand."

"Was this the girl?"

Coach Kompton tilted his head to the side and shrugged.

"Yeah."

Principal Riley leaned across his desk to glare at me.

"I simply want to know, did you open the picture envelope?" He didn't give me time to answer before he asked: "Did you *just* look in it, Courtney?"

I hesitated. I looked at him. I looked at Coach Kompton and the others. I saw the way their eyes squinted as they waited for me to answer. I shook my head.

"No, sir."

CHAPTER

17

Mr. Riley shot Coach Kompton a knowing glance, then turned back to me.

"You didn't open it and just peek in?"

"No," I said, "I didn't *look* in it, I *reached* in and got out the fifteen dollars that I brought from home. But I put the money back."

Mr. Riley seemed a bit startled. He glanced up at Coach Kompton and cocked an eyebrow.

"You see her put it back?"

Coach Kompton shook his head. "It's like I told you yesterday. I saw her take something out, then I heard a ruckus down in the eighth-grade locker section and I went to take care of that."

"I put it back," I insisted again. "Really."

Mr. Riley frowned at me and folded his arms again.

"You took out fifteen dollars?"

"Yes. I was gonna take it home to my daddy and have Mrs. Hooper take my name off the picture list. But I changed my mind and put it back."

"Why did you take it out in the first place?"

I didn't want to tell him. I didn't want them to know about Ben being in jail. I didn't want anyone to know that we were broke because Emily had taken all Daddy's money.

Then I remembered how in third grade, I got sent to the office for hitting Jeff Fonzworth with a rock on the playground. And I remembered how I told Principal Jordan that I didn't do it, and how she believed me and called in Mike Pitts, who had really thrown the rock. And my elementary principal had bragged about how I'd told the truth. She promised me that if I always told the truth, things in life would work out okay.

So I told them the truth. I told them everything, and I just knew that telling the truth would make things all right again.

Junior high isn't elementary. The teachers and the principal have to look after a lot more kids. Or maybe there are more liars in junior high. Or maybe the teachers and principal just don't take as much time to be nice or listen.

When I finished talking and crying, Mrs. Hooper told Mr. Riley that I was a really good student and a "sweet girl" and that she couldn't believe I'd steal anything. Coach Kompton repeated the part about seeing me take some money out of the envelope and not putting it back, *but* that maybe he wasn't watching carefully enough. Mrs. Ingle just stared at me.

Mr. Riley sent the teachers back to their rooms and marched me down to my locker. He had me open it and take everything out. He looked through the locker, picked up all my books, and shook them. He even searched my gym bag.

After that, we went to Mrs. Hooper's room. Mr. Riley made me take all the stuff out of my desk, and he looked through that. Everyone in the room watched and whispered. It didn't take a genius to figure out what was going on. No matter what school you go to, the only reason for the principal to search your desk is because he or she thinks you stole something.

On top of all that, when Mr. Riley left the room, he paused at the door and looked back at me.

"If the money isn't returned by first thing tomorrow morning," he threatened, "I'll have no other choice but to call your father and probably suspend you from school."

I wanted to crawl under my desk and die.

*   *   *

At lunch, Brandy was in my usual chair beside Lacy. Molly Pierce was in the spot at the table where Brandy used to sit. I wandered around aimlessly. Every chair was either full, or when I tried to sit down, I'd find out it was "being saved" for a friend.

I was getting ready to go dump my tray when I heard Judy call my name from across the lunchroom. I sat by her in the chair next to the bin where everybody dumped their garbage.

It wasn't fair!

In the blink of an eye, I'd gone from the table where Lacy and all the popular girls sat to the table by the garbage. Despite the fact that the charges had been dropped against Ben, all the other kids still figured my brother was a jailbird. We were broke, and now everybody in school thought I was a thief. They thought I stole the picture money.

I felt lower than the grungy floor under the garbage dump. I was lower than dirt. Nothing could be worse.

When cheerleading practice was over, I walked to Lacy's car. Just as I got there, she hung her head out the window.

"We have some errands and some shopping to do," she called. "You'll have to catch a ride with somebody else, Courtney."

I blinked and stood there staring at her. Lacy's mom leaned forward to look around her daughter.

"Can you find a ride with someone?" she asked.

I felt numb all over. For some reason, I nodded.

Mrs. Valentine frowned, but she really didn't look all that concerned.

"Are you sure?"

"Yes." My head bobbed up and down again. Lacy motioned with her hands and urged her mother to go. Mrs. Valentine shrugged and I watched as they drove away.

The life—what little there was left—drained out of me. I knew how Daddy felt when he read the note from Emily. It was like every bit of energy, feeling, hope—it all just drizzled into my tennis shoes and leaked out onto the gravel at my feet.

The school bus had already gone. Lacy and her mom had deserted me. Ben was in basketball practice and wouldn't be home for another two hours. I thought about calling Daddy. He was either at the shop or sitting in his chair, looking as dead as I felt. Either way, I simply couldn't bring myself to bother him.

I was all alone. I was empty. I started walking. Ryland Heights was between me and home. It didn't matter. I just didn't care anymore. I walked on heavy feet past some of the bars. No one was outside, but I didn't care whether they were or not. Some old, crusty-looking guys stared at me when I crossed Fifty-ninth and Garland Avenue. I didn't care. A big guy with dark, greasy hair followed me for a block, but he went into a bar. I didn't care.

When the green '65 Mustang full of guys pulled up beside me . . .

I cared.

Suddenly, I was alive again. I was alive and scared to death.

CHAPTER

18

I didn't see the car. Not at first. It was more like a feeling, a presence. A tingling crept across the back of my neck, a feeling like someone was watching me—following me. When I finally glanced over my left shoulder, the '65 Mustang pulled up beside me. A boy in the back and one in the front hung out the window and started whistling at me. For a moment they acted like they were going to climb clear out of the car.

"Hey, girl," one of them called, "you want a ride?"

"Yeah, honey," the one pushing his way out from the back taunted, "come on and hop in here with us. How about a little drink?"

"Yeah, you can sit on my lap and . . ."

My head told me to ignore them. If I pretended

they weren't there, they might go away. My feet
didn't get the message. I started walking faster. The
empty feeling inside me was gone. Every muscle in
my body was tight and tense. Fear raced through
me like the ripples from a rock tossed on the surface
of a calm pool. Without looking at the car, I walked
faster.

Visions of the old films we watched in grade
school flashed through my head—the films about
what to do if a stranger offered you candy or tried to
make you get in his car.

A house. A business with lots of people.

I could run to someone's house and pound on
their door. Maybe a grocery store. I could ask them
to help me.

Only, there weren't any houses. The street where
I walked had only bars or dingy buildings with
boards over the doors and broken windows.

The car stayed right beside me. The boys started
calling out nasty, vulgar things. Things so gross that
my skin began to crawl.

I ran.

Tires squealed and the Mustang shot ahead of
me. At the corner, where I was headed, the door
flew open. One of the boys started to get out.

I darted across the street, behind the car. I was
lucky there were no cars coming because I didn't

even bother to look. I just ran—as hard as I could.

There was an open field. I sprinted through it, dodging the clumps of weeds and tall grass that marked the foundations of old, demolished buildings. I was more than halfway across the field when I saw the car again. I ran to my left—away from it—until it turned the corner at the far end of the block. The moment it turned and started down the street to intercept me, I cut to my right.

The guy driving the Mustang jammed on his brakes. He started to back up, but only got a few feet before a delivery truck came up behind him. When the truck driver started honking, the Mustang went on.

I ran even harder. My heart pounded in my ears. This was my chance. If I could cross the street and make it to a house . . . those apartments over there . . . before the car came around the block . . .

My sides ached. I could hear the rattling in my throat as I gasped for air.

From the corner of my eye, I could see the green Mustang turn at the end of the block as I sprang from the curb into the street.

I gulped a breath and ran.

The tires screamed.

I dodged around a fireplug and darted past a small tree. My lungs felt like they were going to burst. I knew the car was behind me without even looking back. I could hear the roar of the motor.

I ran harder.

Suddenly, I realized where I was.

There was a big apartment complex just across the street. There were six three-story buildings that all looked the same. The buildings were sort of a gray color and needed paint. Some of the screens dangled loose from the windows.

It was No Hope Village. I'd seen it the day Ben and Dexter and I had followed Judy home after Joshua tried to beat her up. The apartment on the end—it was Judy's.

I couldn't breathe. My legs were weak. As the car spun and fishtailed around the corner, I ran harder.

The engine roared. My eyes spun in my head. I was going to faint. I couldn't make it.

Just as I jumped to the curb, the green Mustang slid to a stop. The car almost hit me.

"Judy!" I screamed. Where the breath came from, I don't know. My lungs were empty—exhausted. "Judy! Help!"

The car door creaked open. The boys were so close, I could almost feel a hand grab the back of my blouse.

I stopped at the bottom step. I couldn't go any farther. My legs wouldn't move. My heart pounded in my ears. My chest heaved, then seemed to collapse inside.

"Judy," I gasped.

The screen sprang open. A woman appeared from the darkness inside.

She was a short woman. Tiny—not much bigger than me. She was slender with salt-and-pepper hair that hung limp and lifeless. Her face was angry and wrinkled and mean. So mean that she was almost ugly.

I knew this was Judy's mom, the one that the kids at school called The Witch of No Hope Village.

She glared down at me. Her black eyes seemed to cut through me. They dug inside me like the claws of an angry hawk grabbing hold of its prey.

"Get out of here!" she shrieked. "You get away from my house, RIGHT NOW!!!"

She took a step toward me. It wasn't a step, it was a stomp. Her foot came down so hard it made the loose boards on the porch rattle.

"I mean it. GET!!!"

My knees buckled beneath me. I crumpled to the ground.

CHAPTER

19

I was so scared, exhausted, and helpless, I could hardly lift my head up when she took another pounding step toward me. Tiny as she was, The Witch of No Hope Village seemed to tower above me. Her black eyes . . . those mean, angry eyes . . . well . . .

She wasn't even looking at me. She glared at the green Mustang.

"Ricco Thompson, don't try to hide under that ball cap. I know that's you. I'm gonna call your mama!"

She tilted her head to the side.

"And, Philip Rice. I see you in there, too. The cops were around last week hunting for you. You want me to tell 'em where you are and who you're runnin' with?"

Suddenly, Judy was beside me. Balancing on her cane, she reached down with her free hand and tried to help me up.

"This is my friend from school," she barked at the car. "You punks leave her alone."

"Sorry, Judy," a voice called from behind the tinted windows, "we didn't know she was your friend. She looked older than that."

"Yeah," another voice called, "we wasn't really gonna hurt the kid. We was just messin'."

Judy's mom shooed them away with her hand. "You go mess somewhere else. Scared this child half to death. Now, scat."

The door closed.

"And, Charlie"—The Witch of No Hope Village shook an angry finger at the green Mustang—"when you take off, I don't wanna hear them tires squeal either. You understand me?"

The car pulled away from the curb and crept down the street. Judy and her mother helped me to my feet and took me inside. They plopped me on the couch, and Judy fixed me a glass of water.

"You ought to know better than to walk around this neighborhood by yourself, child," Judy's mom scolded. "You don't live around here. You don't know these people. Why you down here prowling the streets by yourself?"

I told them all about Lacy and her mom running off and leaving me after cheerleading practice. It hurt my insides, and I cried while I was telling them. Then I started to tell Judy how mean everyone had been at school and how they wouldn't let me sit with them. But before I could tell very much, Judy's mom got up from the couch.

"Courtney." She folded her arms and looked at me with those black eyes. "I don't know what it's like at your house. But around here, we got chores to do. We don't have time to bellyache or sit and feel sorry for ourselves. You can go help Judy with her ironing." She pointed toward the back of the apartment. "Soon as that's done, she can walk you home."

Dragging her legs behind her cane, Judy led me down a dark hallway. She pointed at her room. It looked a lot like mine—clean and neat with some stuffed animals on the bed. Her mother's room was at the very end. There was a sewing machine and two ironing boards on either side of a small bed. All the furniture was stacked high with clothes.

"While I'm at school Mama works down at Ryland Heights Dry Cleaners on Fifty-fifth Street. She gets off at three so she can be home when I get here. To make a little extra we take in washing and ironing for people," Judy told me. She pointed to the sewing machine in the corner. "We do some mending, too."

Judy grabbed the iron and sprayed some starch on a shirt she was working on. Her mom sat behind the sewing machine and started mending a pair of slacks. Judy and I talked while she ironed.

When she finished the shirt, I put it on a hanger for her. I folded the stuff that needed folding, but if I did it wrong, Judy showed me how to do it the right way. When we were done, she walked me home.

As we walked through Ryland Heights, I felt safe.

At my house, I paused a moment by the front door. I remembered the beginning of school, when I'd told Emily about the little crippled girl in my class and asked if I could invite her over. I remembered Emily saying how people who lived in No Hope were either blacks or Hispanics or poor white trash, and how she wouldn't let me invite Judy to our home.

Emily was gone.

"You want to come in and play awhile? We can listen to tapes and look through some of my *Seventeens*. Then my brother can drive you home when he gets out of basketball practice."

Judy smiled. "Sure."

*   *   *

After we took Judy home, Ben told me he was glad I had a new friend. He said Lacy was pretty for a twelve-year-old, but . . . how did he say it? . . . "Lacy was sort of cold around the heart. Kind of stuck-up and snooty. I like your new friend. She seems sweet."

I never told Ben about Lacy and how she and the other girls treated me.

When we got home, I *did* tell Daddy about the picture money. He'd been working at the shop instead of sitting in his chair with that blank look on his face. Ben and I both felt like maybe he was doing better, maybe he was going to be all right.

Daddy went to school with me the next morning. He told Mr. Riley that I had never lied to him and that he believed me about the picture money. Mr. Riley said that the coach had seen me reach into the picture-money envelope. He also told Daddy that no one else was around who could have taken the money and he wanted it returned immediately, or he might have to suspend me.

"You're gonna have to get it from someone else," Daddy told him. "If Courtney said she didn't take it, she didn't take it. But if you feel like you need to suspend her for something she didn't do, you go right ahead."

It made me feel good, the way Daddy stood up for me. I just knew he was going to be okay. Emily was a heartless, mean person. She'd hurt him, really bad. But my daddy was going to be okay.

That day, after cheerleading practice, Judy waited for me. When we finished her ironing, she walked me home and I invited her in again.

My daddy wasn't okay. When we walked in, he was sitting in his chair. He had that blank, empty look in his eyes and didn't even say "Hi." I tried to get him to talk to me. I tried to tell him about school and cheerleading practice. He just stared off like a dead man.

Finally, I got right in front of him. I got hold of his chin and made him look at me.

"What's wrong, Daddy?" I pleaded. "Why are you acting like this again?"

His eyes focused on me for only a moment. He handed me a piece of paper, then his gaze drifted away. I looked at the paper. At the top it said:

NOTICE OF FORECLOSURE

I read the thing. But even though I could make out most of the words, I really couldn't understand what it said.

"What is it, Daddy? What does this thing mean?"

Daddy never looked up.

"The bank foreclosed on the shop." He sighed. "I got to go down and get my tools tomorrow. They're closing my shop. Twelve years . . . and they're taking my shop away from me."

CHAPTER

20

Big brothers think they know everything. They really don't.

Ben tried to get Daddy to talk. Daddy wouldn't. Ben tried to get him out of the chair and get him busy doing something. Daddy just sat and stared off into nothing. Finally, Ben gave up.

"Don't worry about it, squirt," he told me, "it's gonna take him time. But time will take care of just about anything. After a while, it'll be better."

Time didn't make it better.

Time didn't get Daddy out of his chair. It didn't get the empty look out of his eyes. Time didn't keep the kids at school from watching me and talking about me behind my back. Although Principal Riley never said any more to me about the picture money, time didn't keep him or Mrs. Ingle from watching me like hawks every time I came near them. Time didn't keep Mrs. Hooper from skipping over my name when it was my turn to be helper. And time didn't make the smell go away from the trash bin beside my chair in the lunchroom.

All through January, it got colder. Not just outside, but inside as well.

Mr. Riley didn't suspend me—at least not yet. Miss Tipton wanted me out of cheerleading. That's what Nancy said. No matter how well I did things or how hard I worked, Miss Tipton was always picking on me or complaining about stuff. Nancy caught me after practice one day and told me that's what she had done to the two eighth-grade girls.

"She got it in for them for some reason," Nancy had said. "Nobody knows why. She just didn't like them or something. But you're good, Courtney. Don't let her get to you. Just hang in there."

Judy, the only bright spot in my whole miserable life, waited for me every day after practice. We would walk to her house and I'd help with the ironing or fold clothes. Sometimes we cleaned the apartment while her mother started supper. When we finished, Judy would either walk me home or we'd go to the basketball court behind No Hope Village and practice free throws, or go to her room and read.

Judy had a ton of books in her room. The first day I ran to her house to get away from the boys in the green Mustang, I'd seen her room, but I hadn't noticed the books. I guess that's because they were in a huge bookshelf behind her door. Most of the books were fiction. She also had travel books and books about trains and ships and all sorts of stuff. One afternoon when we were both kind of quiet and serious, instead of laughing and giggling like we usually did when we were together, I asked her why she had so many books.

"I like 'em," she said flatly.

"I like books, too. But this many?"

Judy shrugged. "Well, Mom doesn't make much at the dry cleaners. We've never been farther north than Dallas. In other words, we don't travel much. And, just in case you haven't noticed"—she pointed down at her legs—"these things don't work too well.

"You ever read a book . . . and . . . all of a sudden you're not reading it anymore? All of a sudden, you're in there. Right in the middle of it. And all the stuff that's happening is happening—not to somebody else, but to you?"

I nodded. Judy smiled.

"That's why. When I'm in a book, I mean a really good book . . . well, I can go anyplace in the whole world. I can see everything. I'm . . . well . . . I'm not a cripple anymore. I can ride a bicycle or a horse. I can play basketball instead of just shooting free throws. I can run barefoot down a sandy beach. I mean . . . *run* like the wind itself."

Judy clamped her lips together and wiped her nose with the back of her thumb. "Imagine that"— she tried to laugh—"me running down a beach?"

I nodded. I could feel the little pools of water at the bottom of my eyes. But before a tear ever had a chance to trickle down my cheek . . .

WHOMP!

Something slammed against the side of my head. I jerked so hard I almost fell off the bed. Startled, I looked around.

WHOMP!

I jerked again. Blinked.

Judy sat, smiling at me. There was a pillow in her hand.

"What are you looking so gloomy about?" A mischievous twinkle sparked her eyes. "You couldn't run down the beach either. You'd probably trip, land on a seashell, and give yourself another black eye."

Then she hit me again.

The only thing I could do was defend myself. I grabbed a pillow and whomped her back. First thing I knew, we were pounding each other, tumbling around the bed and laughing so hard I thought I was going to wet my pants. We might have even busted one of her feather pillows if it hadn't been for . . .

"That's enough of that, ladies!"

Mrs. Baird stood in the open doorway. There was a stern, angry look on her face. Still, I couldn't help but notice the twinkle in her eye—just like the one in Judy's.

"There are chores to be done. If you two are going to roughhouse and tumble around, fine. Just do your ironing first and go outside afterward to wrestle."

She turned to leave, then suddenly stopped. Spinning back to face us, she dug in the pocket of the white apron she wore. She pulled something out and came toward me. "Almost forgot." She held out her hand. "Mr. Metcalf finally paid me for his shirts and slacks. Here."

I took what she handed me and looked at it. There were seven one-dollar bills and two quarters.

"What's this?"

Mrs. Baird frowned. "Just told you. Mr. Metcalf paid for his stuff. That's your part of it."

I looked at the money in my hand and shook my head.

"Fifty cents a shirt and a dollar each on the slacks. You did three pair of pants and nine of the shirts. That comes to seven-fifty."

Shaking my head, I tried to hand the money back to her.

"I can't take this. I was just helping Judy. I wasn't expecting to be paid or . . ."

"Don't care what you were expecting," Mrs. Baird huffed. "You work, you get paid. That's the way things operate around here."

"But . . ."

"No buts. You did the work. There's no argument or debate about it. That's just the way it is. Now both of you get to work. I want your chores finished so you can get out of the house. You're making too much racket."

School was miserable, but I could almost survive, because as soon as school was over, I got to go to Judy's. I appreciated the money. There wasn't much, but it would help with groceries and stuff. Mostly, I looked forward to being with Judy and her mom.

Home was a different matter. Sooner or later, I

always had to go home. Ben was okay, and I was managing to get through the days. Daddy was the big problem.

He'd given up. All he did was sit in his chair like a zombie or something. He didn't even help Ben or me with the housekeeping or cooking. Now and then, he'd come to the table at suppertime. Mostly, Ben or I took his plate to him. Sometimes he ate, sometimes he didn't. Ben tried to talk to him. Even Dexter's dad came over and encouraged him to come and work at the police garage with him. Daddy just sat.

Ben dropped out of basketball and got a job busing tables at Ding Ho's Chinese restaurant. That and the money he'd been saving for a new car when he graduated from high school was barely enough to pay bills and buy food. By the end of January, Daddy's face was all drawn and he looked like he'd lost a bunch of weight. It was like he was wasting away a little at a time, and soon there'd be nothing left.

I hated Daddy for that. I hated Lacy Valentine and all the other brats she hung around with. I hated Emily for taking all our money and running off with some guy who couldn't hold a candle to my daddy. I hated Ben for not being able to say or do anything to keep Daddy from wasting away into nothing.

Mostly, I hated me. It seemed like all I could do was feel sorry for myself.

But by late February, I didn't even hate me anymore.

I just didn't care.

It didn't matter that the world was a rotten place. I became accustomed to the whispers behind my back and being shunned when I neared the "popular table" where I used to sit in the lunchroom. I almost accepted the stench from the trash bin. At home, I got in the habit of going straight to my room when I came in from school, so I wouldn't have to watch my daddy fade away. I didn't care if Miss Tipton yelled at me in cheerleading practice or if none of the kids at school liked me anymore. I got used to the empty, cold, lonely feeling that filled my insides.

I just didn't care.

If it hadn't been for Judy, I don't know what I would have done. I might have jumped out in front of a car or dropped out of school. Judy was my best friend. I'd never had a friend like her—and probably never would again.

*   *   *

Then on February 25, even Judy left me.

I remember the day because it was the day we had a snow-and-ice storm. In our part of Texas it hardly ever snows, so I always remember when it happens.

I remember the day because when I came out of cheerleading practice, Judy, my best friend, wasn't there waiting for me.

I remember the day—the exact date—because it was the day that changed my life forever.

CHAPTER

21

Lacy was climbing to the very top of the pyramid when the whole thing crumbled. We all fell.

"Courtney," Miss Tipton huffed, "if you can't keep your mind on practice, you might as well not even be in here. Why don't you just . . ."

Nancy stepped between us.

"Miss Tipton, it wasn't Courtney," she said. "Lacy kicked Beth in the side of the head when she was climbing up. It wasn't Courtney's fault."

Miss Tipton glared at her.

"Forget it," she snapped. "I've got a teachers' meeting this afternoon. If you all are going to flop around on the floor instead of working on this routine . . . well, just forget the whole thing. I'm going to the meeting."

She stormed off and left us standing there with our mouths open. Nancy tried to talk to me. I told her I didn't care. Even Beth apologized for the way Miss Tipton had blamed me for something she did. I told her it didn't matter. Lacy left. I didn't care about that either. When I got outside, Judy wasn't there. The sky was as gray and bleak as my heart. I walked around the corner to see if Judy was behind the wall, trying to stay out of the strong north wind and the snow. When I didn't find my friend, I went around the other corner. She wasn't there either, so I started walking.

The ground was slippery. A thin layer of ice had formed under the big wet flakes of snow. I slipped a couple of times and had to throw my arms out, like a circus performer on a high wire, to keep my balance.

The streets were almost empty. There weren't many cars and even the drunks, who hung around some of the bars, had gone inside to get out of the cold and snow.

A flake landed on my nose. I crossed my eyes and looked down at the little lacy crystal as it melted.

"Maybe Judy went home," I told it. "We weren't in cheerleading practice very long, but it's really cold and nasty out here. Maybe she got cold and . . ."

Another snowflake landed on my eyelash. I blinked.

". . . or maybe she just doesn't like me anymore."

I decided to stop by her house on my way home.
I would ask her why she left me.

But, no matter what she might say . . . well, I
guess it just didn't matter.

The door opened, then the screen swung wide
when I stepped on the porch of the old gray-looking
apartment.

"Get in here, child!" As always, Mrs. Baird's voice
was stern and grumpy. "Come on in 'fore you freeze
to death."

She stepped aside. I stomped my feet and walked
past her. It still amazed me how tiny she was. The
way the kids at school talked about The Witch of No
Hope Village, I'd always expected someone taller
and much bigger. Mrs. Baird never hesitated to yell
at kids who were doing something wrong. Maybe
the threats to call their parents or to call the police
or the way she faced down grown-ups who were
twice as big as she—maybe that's what earned her
the nickname.

I wiped my shoes on the rug a couple of times
before I stepped onto the linoleum.

"I need to see Judy," I said. "Is she in her room?"

Mrs. Baird frowned.

"I thought she was with you."

I shook my head and frowned back at her.

"No. I thought she came home. I couldn't find her at school. I better go back for her."

As I started for the door, Judy's mother got hold of the doorjamb. She leaned out so she could see down to the corner where we always crossed. Her arm was in the way, so I waited.

"No, here she comes."

For an instant, I almost thought I saw The Witch of No Hope Village smile. I leaned down and peeked under her arm. I guess I missed Judy at school. She must have been following me all the way. I never bothered to look back, and if she had called to me, the blustery wind and the crunch of the ice beneath my feet must have kept her words from my ears.

Balancing on her cane in front and dragging her legs behind her, Judy walked briskly to the corner. Her little stocking cap was caked with snow. Just as she turned to come down the sidewalk, her cane slipped on the ice.

She fell.

She fell hard! Judy usually managed to twist around and land on her bottom when she fell. Sometimes, she'd catch herself with her hands. This time, when the cane slipped on the ice, she went down face-first. She landed on her nose and chest.

I tried to push my way under Mrs. Baird's arm.

"I'll go get her," I said.

Only, Mrs. Baird dropped her hand from the doorjamb and caught my shoulder.

"No."

"But she's hurt."

"She'll get up."

With a jerk of my shoulder, I shook her hand away and tried to slip behind her.

"It's icy. It's slippery. She can't . . ."

Mrs. Baird pushed against me so I couldn't get around.

"She'll get up!" she repeated.

No wonder people called her The Witch of No Hope Village. I couldn't believe she wouldn't let me go help Judy. Her daughter had fallen. The way she'd landed, she might have a bloody nose, or maybe her ribs were busted. Still, this nasty old witch wouldn't let me get past her to go help her own daughter.

I pressed my cheek against her arm where it blocked my path, so I could see down to the corner. Judy lay there for a long, long time. The snow began to collect on the back of her jacket in a thin white film. Finally, she rolled over and sat up.

She put her cane beside her with the rubber tip on the ground and the crook behind her right shoulder. But when she tried to walk her hands up the shaft, like I'd seen her do so many times before, the cane slipped. She tried again.

"She can't do it," I pleaded, almost crying. "It's too slippery. She just can't."

"She can! She's got to!"

For the first time, I took my eyes from Judy and looked at the woman beside me. She was so small, we were almost eye level. I looked at her eyes. They weren't black and angry like they were when she yelled at people around the apartments for getting into stuff they weren't supposed to. They weren't black and stern like they were when she told me to quit feeling sorry for myself and go help Judy with her chores.

The Witch of No Hope Village had brown eyes. Soft eyes that were full of worry and love as she watched her daughter slipping and struggling on the ice. Her chin quivered.

"Why?" I asked. My voice was almost a whisper. "Why does she have to get up by herself?"

Mrs. Baird never took her eyes from her daughter.

"When she was five, the doctors told me she'd never get up again. She'd be confined to a wheelchair. She got up!" She forced her chin to stop quivering by jutting it forward. "When she was seven, they told me she'd have to use a wheelchair and probably be in it the rest of her life. They also told me she'd more than likely have to be in an institution by the time she was twelve. SHE GOT UP!"

"But this is different. There's ice and . . ."

"No," she barked, "it's no different! This old world is always knocking you down. With Judy . . . the way she is . . . well, she's gonna get knocked down more than most." She glanced at me for only an instant, then looked back at her daughter. "The only lesson Judy ever has to learn in this life is how to get up. It's the only lesson any of us can't afford to forget. Judy WILL GET UP!"

She clamped her lips together so tight that her nose and her chin even turned white. Beside me, I could feel her straining and pushing. It was like every ounce of her being was out there with her daughter—pulling, fighting, doing everything she could to help her get up.

Judy fell again. She tried and fell once more. Then she reached out and twisted the rubber tip from her cane. She stuffed it into her pocket. She jabbed the wooden point into the ice.

This time . . . it held. She walked herself up the cane, dusted the snow from her jeans, and headed toward the house.

I looked over at Mrs. Baird. A single tear leaked

from her eye and rolled silently down her cheek. It wasn't a tear of sorrow or pity. Her eyes weren't filled with worry or pain. The look in her eyes was love and the little tear was one of pride and hope.

A chill started down deep in the small of my back. It raced up my spine and spread across my shoulders and arms. The chill ran clear to the tips of my fingers.

Suddenly I realized Judy Baird wasn't the little sixth-grade crippled girl—*I was!*

CHAPTER

22

At school, I waited outside the library until the meeting was finally over. When the doors opened wide and the teachers came streaming out, I spotted Miss Tipton and dodged around a couple of people to reach her.

"Miss Tipton," I said, tugging at the sleeve of her blouse, "I need to speak with you a moment."

Following the flow of the crowd, she took a few more steps before she stopped.

"It's snowing out there. I need to get home."

"It'll just take a second. Please?"

She looked irritated, but she moved with me to stand by the wall. I spotted Mrs. Hooper and went after her.

"Courtney," Miss Tipton called behind me, "I don't have all day . . ."

I didn't hear the rest of what she said. I dodged my way around people and stopped right in front of Mrs. Hooper. She looked a bit startled to see me at school, then she smiled. "Hi, Courtney, what are you doing here this late?"

"I need to speak with you and Miss Tipton. It will only take a moment. There's just something I *have* to tell both of you."

She followed me to the wall where I had left Miss Tipton. I waited a moment while most of the teachers cleared out of the hall near where we stood. Then I looked at both of them, and took a deep breath.

"For almost two months," I began, "the kids and teachers have been talking about me and pointing at me in the halls. First, it was because my brother got arrested. Everybody knew about it. Then, when the police dropped all the charges and let him go, you started watching me because you thought I stole the stupid picture money."

I turned to look Miss Tipton square in the eye.

"Lately, no matter how hard I work or how good I do, you're not happy with me in cheerleading."

Miss Tipton twisted her mouth to the side.

"So?"

"So, griping at me about something isn't going to work." I forced my voice to stay calm and soft. "If you want me out of cheerleading, then call my dad or take me to the office and tell Mr. Riley that I'm no good or whatever. But quit riding my back. I'm not going to *QUIT!* You're gonna have to throw me out."

I turned to Mrs. Hooper.

"I liked you a lot, Mrs. Hooper. You're one of the nicest teachers at Blyle. But it really hurts my feelings that you don't trust me anymore. It's just not fair that I don't ever get to be helper. If you can't treat me like the rest of the class, maybe you should ask Mr. Riley to move me to another room."

With that, I turned and left. I didn't say another word. I didn't storm off. I didn't look back.

"Just a minute, young lady!" Mrs. Hooper's voice was stern.

I kept walking.

"Courtney, wait. Please." Mrs. Hooper caught me by the shoulders and turned me around so I had to face her. "There's something in the room I want to show you. Come on. Please."

Miss Tipton, mumbling something to herself, trotted down the hall. I walked with my teacher to our room. She opened the top desk drawer, pulled out her grade book, and motioned me to stand beside her while she thumbed through some of the pages.

"This is my helpers' sheet," she said, pointing at one of the pages. "Your name is right here. Week after next, it will be your turn. You have not been skipped. With as many students as I have it simply takes a while to cycle everyone through." She closed her book and held me by the shoulders. "I'm sorry you've been miserable and felt as if no one trusted you. I don't believe you stole the money. I never did. In fact, I told Mr. Riley that and . . ."

"But Mr. Riley and his secretary are always watching me in the halls," I interrupted.

Mrs. Hooper brushed my comment away with a wave of her hand. "Mr. Riley and his secretary are always watching *everybody* in the halls. I don't think he watches you any closer than any of the other kids. And, if he does . . . well, you've got to understand his point of view. Coach Kompton saw you reach into the envelope. He didn't see you put the money back because he was distracted by some boys messing around the lockers. Mrs. Ingle and Mr. Riley were inside the inner office and didn't see you. Even Greg Bowlin says he didn't see anything. He said all he saw was you putting the envelope on the desk."

Frowning, I tilted my head so far to the side, my ear almost touched my shoulder.

"What did you say about Greg?"

"Huh?"

"You said Greg saw me."

Mrs. Hooper nodded. "Yes. He told Mr. Riley that he saw you put the envelope on the desk, but he didn't see you open it or anything else."

I shook my head.

"But Greg wasn't in there."

"He wasn't?"

"No. I remember you sent him to the office for playing in the drinking fountain, but when I got there the office was empty. I figured Greg was already in with Mr. Riley."

Mrs. Hooper put her elbow on the desk and rested her chin in her hand. She sat there a long time, kind of staring off at the wall like she was trying to remember. Finally, she looked back at me and shook her head.

"No, Mr. Riley and Mrs. Ingle were both in his office with a parent. Greg told Mr. Riley he saw you while he was waiting in the chair by the door. You didn't see him in the chair?"

I shook my head.

"The office was empty?"

I nodded.

"You're sure?"

I nodded again.

Suddenly, Mrs. Hooper was on her feet. "That little sneak."

"Who? What?"

"Greg," she answered. "He told Mr. Riley he saw you put the envelope on the table. But you say the office was empty—you didn't see Greg. So that means the little stinker wasn't sitting in the chair as he was supposed to. He was up prowling around the office or hiding some place. That little . . ."

She slapped her palm against her leg. I followed her through the door and down the hall. I practically had to run to keep up with her.

"I need to talk to Mr. Riley," she said over her shoulder. "I just hope he hasn't already left."

The office was locked. I chased Mrs. Hooper outside. We got to the parking lot, just in time to see Mr. Riley's car slipping and sliding up the street.

"First thing tomorrow morning, I'm going to get Greg and see if we can't straighten this thing out. You need a ride home?"

I looked up at her and smiled.

As we drove toward my house, Mrs. Hooper said that there was probably no way we could prove that Greg took the money. She also said that she usually didn't talk about her students with other students, but since I'd been through so much—well, both of us knew what Greg was like and even if we couldn't prove it . . . well . . .

We stopped for the light at Fifty-eighth and Timber Creek Drive. Mrs. Hooper's car stalled. We

talked awhile longer, and when she stopped for another light on Forty-second and Woolridge, her motor died again. This time she had trouble getting it
to start.

"Darned thing's been doing that since this morning." She turned the key and popped her foot up
and down on the gas pedal. "I don't know what's
wrong with the stupid . . ."

Cars started honking behind us. She ground the
starter, and the motor finally kicked over.

It sounded like the idle arm to the carburetor was
set too low. I started to tell her. Suddenly, I jerked.
I clamped my lips shut, stopping myself.

"My daddy's a pretty good mechanic," I told her.
"If you could wait a minute when we get to my
house, maybe he could help."

She nodded.

Mrs. Hooper's car stalled at every light and stop
sign. When she pulled up in front of my house, it
completely died.

"I'll be right back," I called as I leaped out and
scurried for the house.

Daddy was sitting in his chair with that blank look
on his face. His eyes were far away and empty.

"Daddy," I said, "my teacher brought me home,
but her car keeps dying every time she stops. Can
you see what's wrong with it?"

He didn't look up.

"Daddy? I need help. Please get up and . . ."

He didn't even blink.

"GET UP!!!"

I screamed the words so loud, he jumped. Ben was home and came scurrying from the other end of the house.

Daddy's blank eyes focused on me.

"Huh! What?"

I grabbed his arm and yanked.

"I said, GET UP!"

I practically pulled him from the chair. Startled, he looked around and blinked.

"What is it? What's wrong?"

"Mrs. Hooper, my teacher, her car won't run. It dies every time we stop. I don't know what's wrong with it. She can't get home unless you help me fix it."

Ben and I put Daddy's coat on him. Ben grabbed his own coat and we went outside. Daddy and Mrs. Hooper started her car. He listened to the engine, and it took him about two seconds to figure out what was wrong. He got a Phillips-head screwdriver from his truck and adjusted the idle-arm screw to the motor. Mrs. Hooper thanked us and headed home.

Daddy started back to the house, but I grabbed his arm.

"My car next."

"Huh?"

"My car. The one you promised to give me when I turn sixteen," I said, dragging him toward the garage. "We put that new carburetor kit in and it still won't run. Now I'm gonna have to pull the rings and plugs. But I'm not strong enough to get the plugs out by myself. You're gonna have to help."

"But it's snowing out. The garage is cold . . ."

"I don't care. You're my daddy and I need your help. Now, come on!"

All three of us worked on the Corvette. While we worked, we talked. For the first time in a long, long while, I think my daddy listened.

When I was little, I used to think my daddy was the smartest, bravest, most perfect man in the whole wide world. I loved him.

Now, I knew Daddy was just a man. Kind of an ordinary man. Like everybody else, he wasn't perfect. He made mistakes. I loved him even more, now.

When we finished with the car, he didn't go back to his recliner. He fixed us all some hot chocolate and we sat at the kitchen table.

Daddy folded his arms and frowned across the table at me.

"You couldn't figure out that it was the idle-arm adjustment on your teacher's car?"

I shrugged and stirred my hot chocolate.

"You didn't have to get me to fix *that*. You knew good and well what was wrong and . . ."

"I wasn't sure," I lied.

"Yeah, right." Daddy snorted.

I put my spoon down and scrunched my eyes. "I figured you needed to get up. You've sat around long enough feeling sorry for yourself. It's time to get off your tail and get back to work."

"You sound just like your mother." Daddy's chin sort of jutted out. Then his look softened. He looked at me sort of sideways. He blinked, scooted back in his chair, and looked at me again. "I never realized it before," he sighed, "you're starting to look a lot like her, too."

It was the nicest thing Daddy ever said to me.

CHAPTER

23

When I got up the next morning, I threw the musk bath soap that Lacy had given me at Christmas in the trash. Vel smelled fresh and clean and nice. Daddy was already awake when I dressed and came to the kitchen. He wasn't sitting in his chair watching TV. He had fixed breakfast for Ben and me.

"Got your Sunday-go-to-meetin' clothes on," Ben noted as he sat down to start eating. "What's the occasion?"

Daddy poured himself a cup of coffee. "Oh, nothin'. Just thought I'd drop by the bank and see if there was any way I could talk them into extending my loan so I could get my shop back."

I noticed Ben sort of nibble at his bottom lip. He didn't say anything, so I did.

"And what if you can't get your shop back?"

Daddy shrugged and stared deep into his coffee cup, like something was in there.

"Well, there's always Paul Langley and the police garage. I mean, it's not like having my own garage, but it would pay the bills and the hours aren't too bad. What do you two think?"

Ben peeked up from his scrambled eggs. We both winked.

That morning, Mr. Riley brought a new student to our room. Her name was Pamela Franz-mathis, and she and her brother had just moved here. When Mr. Riley left, he took Greg Bowlin with him.

Greg never came back.

I was waiting in line for my tray when Mr. Riley came into the lunchroom. He looked around, kind of searching the room.

"Is Courtney Brown in here?" he yelled across the cafeteria.

Everybody looked up, but they were still noisy.

"You guys get quiet," he roared. "Is Courtney in here?"

I raised my hand and waved.

Mr. Riley could have come across the room to talk to me. Instead, he stayed where he was. I guess he wanted everybody to hear what he had to say.

"Miss Brown," he began, "I've come down to apologize to you. Earlier this morning, I visited with a young man who was sent to the office on the morning you brought the picture money down. I found out that he was hiding under the secretary's desk and *he* was the one who stole the money."

The lunchroom was dead quiet.

"I sincerely apologize for accusing you of taking the money, Miss Brown. I am very, *very* sorry. If there's anything I can ever do to make it up to you . . ."

Everyone turned to look at me. All I could do was sort of shrug and shake my head. When he left, the buzz that started was almost deafening. Mr. Riley never apologized to anybody. From what I could hear of the conversation around me, it was a regular first for Blyle Junior High.

I got my tray and Judy followed me toward our spot. As we passed Lacy's table, she hopped up and pulled an empty chair out.

"Courtney." She looked at me with that oozy-sweet smile. "Why don't you come sit with us?"

"Where's Judy going to sit?"

She sort of looked around. "We've only got one empty chair. Maybe . . ."

"Forget it." I walked past her. But about halfway to our regular spot, I saw the new kid—Pamela Franzmathis. She and a boy I didn't recognize were already sitting in Judy's and my spot by the trash dump.

Judy bumped into the back of me.

"The new kids are in our spot," I told her over my shoulder.

We stood, looking around for someplace to sit. There were a lot of empty chairs in the lunchroom, but no two were together. We just sort of froze there, looking lost and stupid.

"Courtney. Judy. Over here."

We looked behind us. Nancy Osoki waved at us from the seventh-grade side of the lunchroom. She pointed down. "We've got a couple of empty chairs. Come on and sit with us."

Another silence swept through the lunchroom. It was another first for Blyle Junior High. No sixth grader had *ever* been invited to sit with the seventh grade.

Nancy and her friends made us feel like we belonged. We talked and laughed and giggled. And as I sat there, I thought to myself: "Courtney Brown, you got the world by the tail."

A little smile tugged at the corners of my mouth.

*　　*　　*

When we went to empty our trays, somehow Judy and Nancy got ahead of me. I ended up stuck behind a whole bunch of people, so they waited for me by the door. Pamela Franzmathis, the new girl in our class, and the boy she sat with— I guess it was her brother— were right ahead of me in line.

"One of the kids at lunch said that Courtney Brown, the one with the blond hair, is a cheerleader. She's real popular," the boy said.

"Yeah, that's what I heard," Pamela answered. "She is kind of cute. I just can't figure why she hangs around with that poor little crippled girl."

"Yeah," her brother agreed. "I hear she won't even help her up when she falls down and . . ."

Suddenly, his eyes flashed when he saw me standing right behind them. He gave a little jerk of his head. Pamela glanced back and her mouth flopped so wide, I was afraid the flies that hung around the tray dump would buzz in.

"Oh, hi." She smiled sheepishly. Quickly, she turned toward her brother. "Maybe crippled isn't the right word. Maybe handicapped would be better." She kind of glanced at me out of the side of one eye and cocked her eyebrow.

I started to tell them that Judy wasn't a "poor little crippled girl"—she was just fine. And I started to tell them that as far as being "handicapped," sometimes people like me, who think they're "normal," are really the ones with a handicap. I started to tell them how Judy had taught me how to get up and keep going when the world knocked me down and that the reason that I "hung around" with her was because she was nice enough to put up with me, and I enjoyed spending time with Judy and her mother.

I started to tell them all that and more, only . . . well . . . there are just some things people have to figure out for themselves. So . . .

"She's my friend." I said politely. "Her name's Judy. But if that's too hard to remember, crippled or handicapped is fine. It doesn't matter."

About the Author

BILL WALLACE was a principal and physical education teacher for ten years at the same elementary school he attended as a child in his hometown of Chickasha, Oklahoma. The character of Judy Baird in *True Friends* was inspired by one of his own very brave students. On the family farm, Bill helps his wife and son care for their four dogs, three cats, and two horses. He lectures at schools around the country, answers mail from his readers, and, of course, works on his books. His novels have won sixteen state awards and made the master lists in twenty-four states.